Genovia

A Olivia's Room
B Grandmère's Room
C Mia's Room
D Rocky's Room
E Main Staircase
F Throne Room
G Ballroom
H Billiard Room
I Dad's Office
J Hall of Portraits
K Kitchens

L Royal Dining Room
M Royal Genovian Guards
N Library
O Tennis Courts
P Stables
Q Royal Genovian Gardens
R Royal Genovian Academy
S Downtown Genovia
T Beach
U Royal Genovian Yacht Club

From the Notebooks of a Middle School Princess

Royal Crown

Written & illustrated by

MEG CABOT

SQUARE
FISH

Feiwel & Friends ♛ New York

SQUARE
FISH

An imprint of Macmillan Publishing Group, LLC
120 Broadway, New York, NY 10271
mackids.com

ISBN 978-1-250-30868-9 (paperback)   ISBN 978-1-250-11153-1 (ebook)

Originally published in the United States by Feiwel and Friends
First Square Fish edition, 2019
Book designed by April Ward
Square Fish logo designed by Filomena Tuosto

1   3   5   7   9   10   8   6   4   2

AR: 5.2 / LEXILE: 810L

By command of the
Royal Palace of Genovia

You are invited to be present
At 1:00 P.M., Thursday,
the 31st day of December

For the Coronation of Her Royal Highness

Princess Amelia Mignonette
Grimaldi Thermopolis Renaldo

The Throne Room
Reception to Follow
Dress: Formal

Monday, December 28
11:30 A.M.
Royal Pool

It's three days before my sister's royal coronation . . . the first coronation of a female ruler in Genovia in *two centuries*!

I should be having fun—especially since it's winter break, my best friend, Nishi, is visiting from America, and I get to be *in* the coronation ceremony.

But instead I'm being forced to entertain my snobby cousin Lady Luisa Ferrari because her grandmother, the baroness, is in Biarritz with her new gentleman friend.

"I'm bored," Luisa keeps saying.

"*You're* the one who said you wanted to work on your tan," I remind her. We're stretched out in the winter sun on chaise longues next to the pool, which is heated. But still.

"How can you be bored staying in a *royal palace*?" Nishi wants to know. She doesn't mind hanging by the pool, because even though it's only seventy degrees in Genovia right now, it's thirty-five and snowing in New Jersey, where Nishi's visiting from. "They have *everything* here: tennis courts, horseback riding, sailing, mani-pedis, a state-of-the-art home theater, all the food you can eat, prepared by a *five-star* chef—"

"Yes, but hello." Luisa holds up her phone. "The cell service? Horrible."

"What do you expect from a building that was constructed in medieval times?" I ask. "The walls had to be made three feet thick in order to keep out invading marauders."

"Yes, but now they're keeping out my cell phone service provider." Lady Luisa adjusts her floppy hat.

She wants to tan on her body, not her face. "It's no wonder the duke hasn't been able to reach me."

The duke. That's all Luisa ever talks about, her boyfriend, the Duke of Marborough.

I have a boyfriend, too—well, a friend-who-is-a-boy—but I don't talk about him all the time.

And I highly doubt that the reason Luisa hasn't heard from her boyfriend is because of the palace's thick walls. More likely it's because they're in another one of their fights. All Luisa and the duke ever do is fight, usually over the duke's refusal to do anything except play video games. Which would be all right if Luisa played video games, too, but she doesn't.

"You know, Luisa," I can't help pointing out, "you're living through one of the most momentous occasions in Genovian history. My sister's coronation on Thursday is going to be attended by over two hundred heads of state and televised worldwide—"

"Oh my God, I know," Luisa says with a yawn. "You've only mentioned it a million times. Could you please pass me the sunscreen?"

It's not really my cousin's fault that she's so rude. She actually has a pretty rough home life. Her parents are getting divorced and, according to my friend Princess Komiko, her mom and dad are fighting over who *isn't* going to get custody of Lady Luisa.

That's why Luisa lives with her grandmother in the first place, a grandmother who is always jetting off to places like Biarritz with new gentlemen friends.

"I don't understand why your sister even has to have a coronation ceremony, Olivia," Nishi says. "Isn't she already a princess?"

It's natural that Nishi would be confused about this, since she's from the US and hasn't been getting the endless lessons on the coronation that we have here in Genovia, both in school and on the nightly news.

"Of course she's already a princess," I say. "We both are, since our dad is a prince. But Dad is abdicating—which means giving up the crown—so that he can spend more time with me and Rocky. So on Thursday, at the coronation, Mia will formally take over the throne from my dad."

"Oh." Nishi adjusts her sunglasses. "But then why isn't she becoming a queen?"

I sigh. Royal life is complicated.

"Because Genovia is a principality," I explain, "which means it's ruled by either a prince or a princess, not a king or a queen."

"Um, technically, it's not ruled by either," Luisa says in a waspish voice. "Genovians have a prime minister. The royal family doesn't actually make any laws. Their role is only symbolic. So it's not like Princess Mia will actually ever *do* anything once she's crowned."

I suck in my breath, shocked.

But before I can tell Lady Luisa how rude she's

being, Rocky, my little stepbrother, comes bursting into the royal gardens, running at full speed, my miniature poodle, Snowball, barking at his heels.

"Olivia!" he shrieks. "They're here! They're finally here!"

"Good grief," Luisa says, lowering her sunglasses to get a better look at him. "What's *his* problem?"

What's yours? I want to ask her, even though I already know.

"What's here, Rocky?" I ask him instead, when he skids to a stop in front of us.

"The Robe of State," he pants. "And the royal crown!"

No more hanging out at the pool with my rude cousin for me! I've got a crown to inspect.

Monday, December 28
1:30 P.M.
Royal Sitting Room

I knew something was going to go wrong—something besides my having to entertain my awful cousin Lady Luisa all day (and night), I mean. It seems like my family can never have an ordinary, universally televised state function without it turning into a disaster.

And now it looks as if the coronation will be no exception.

Normally the royal crown is in a bulletproof glass case in the palace museum with all the other crown jewels.

But because my sister, Mia, will be wearing it later this week for the coronation, it was sent out for cleaning.

Now it's back and has been brought upstairs to our living quarters so that Paolo, the royal beauty stylist, can figure out which of Mia's hairdos will best keep it in place.

We were all standing around admiring it . . . and trying it on, even though the royal crown isn't supposed to be worn by anyone except the reigning monarch.

But Mia said it was okay, because when will we ever have another chance to try on the *actual royal crown of Genovia*?

I have a tiara, of course (made of real diamonds!), but it's not a crown since it doesn't go all the way around my head . . . and it's certainly not *the* royal crown of Genovia.

"It's so heavy!" Luisa cried, when it was her turn to try it on.

"It weighs seven pounds," Mia informed us from the couch, where she was bouncing Baby Prince

Frank, the fussiest of the twins, in her arms. "So you can imagine how much your neck would hurt after wearing it for a few hours."

"And it's worth over twenty million dollars," my dad added. "So please be careful with it."

"My neck doesn't hurt a bit." Lady Luisa stared at her reflection in the mirror. "I could wear it all day. I've never worn anything worth twenty million dollars before."

"Believe me," Mia said, "one of the first things I did when I found out I was a princess was try to get Dad to sell the crown and donate the money to the orphans of Genovia."

"*Pfuit!*" said Grandmère scornfully. "The orphans of Genovia don't need our money. They all have trust funds."

"The sapphires really bring out the blue in my eyes," Luisa said, admiring her reflection some more.

"Yes," I said. "They do. Now, why don't you give someone else a turn?" She'd been wearing the crown for almost five minutes.

"What's that?" Luisa asked instead of surrendering the crown, pointing at a red velvet cape that was hanging on a dressmaker's dummy in the corner.

"Oh," I said. "That's the Robe of State. It's two hundred years old. It just got back from the cleaners, too."

"And a good thing it did," Rocky said, "because that skunk-fur trim smelled like farts."

"That trim is most certainly not skunk fur," Grandmère said tartly. "It is Alpine ermine, and extremely rare. And the robe did not smell of flatulence, it smelled of mildew from having had champagne spilled on it the last time it was worn." She gave Dad the evil eye, which he pretended not to notice. "The Robe of State plays almost as important a role in the coronation as the crown. It is worn by the reigning monarch every time there's an important state function, such as a coronation, the opening of Parliament, or the bachelor party of one's brand-new son-in-law, apparently."

"And traditionally," Dad said quickly, "the youngest royal in the family always carries the robe's train. And since Princess Elizabeth and Prince Frank aren't old enough yet even to crawl, Olivia is the one upon whom this formidable responsibility has fallen."

I tried to look modest when Nishi smiled at me, impressed.

"It's no different than when we carried Mia's train at her wedding," I said with a shrug.

But it *is* different, since the beautiful lace train of my sister's wedding dress was a lot lighter than the Genovian Robe of State's twenty-foot train. I know, since I've already lifted the robe a few times for practice. I have no idea how Mia's going to get down the entire length of the throne room in that heavy thing, even with my help.

We'd finally wrestled the crown from Luisa—who really didn't want to give it up—and were trying it on Snowball just for laughs when a footman knocked on the door with a letter that had just been delivered by special courier.

I didn't think anything of it at the time. My sister gets letters delivered by special courier all the time. She's about to be the reigning princess of Genovia, after all, even if some people (Lady Luisa) don't think that's a big deal.

But this letter was different. I could tell by my sister's face after she opened it.

"Oh no," Mia said.

"What is it?" her husband, Michael, asked. He was trying to bounce both twins in his arms. All the twins do all day (when they're not sleeping or eating) is cry. Having a newborn twin niece and nephew is not as much fun as I thought it would be. "More yes RSVPs to the coronation?"

"Why does everyone wait until the last minute to respond to invitations?" Grandmère asked. "It's the height of rudeness."

"No," Mia said, reading the letter. "It's much worse than that. It's about our cousin, Prince René Alberto."

"Oh," I said. "Is he the one who keeps getting arrested for illegal offshore gambling?"

"No," Mia said. "He's the one who keeps contesting my right to the throne. And now he's doing it again.

Only this time he's filed a cease and desist order in an attempt to stop the coronation."

"What?" I almost dropped the royal crown, which could have been a disaster. It's very old, and the jewels aren't really screwed in that tightly. "How can he do that?"

"He's claiming that his eight-year-old son has more right to the throne of Genovia than I do."

"On what possible grounds?" Michael asked, looking outraged on his wife's behalf.

"And since when does René have a son, anyway?" Grandmère demanded. "I thought he and that horrid wife of his had a daughter. I distinctly remember the birth announcement. They named her Morgan. I sent her an Add-A-Pearl necklace, and every birthday since, I've been sending a pearl, not that they've ever thanked me."

"Morgan can be a girl's or a boy's name, Grandmère," Rocky pointed out. "And boys can like pearl necklaces."

"Well, evidently Morgan doesn't," Mia said. "Or at

least not enough, because his father is now demanding that I hand over the crown instead."

My stepmother, Helen Thermopolis, shook her head. "What possible reason could Cousin René have to think that his son has more of a claim to the throne than you do, Mia? Is it because he's a boy? How typically sexist!"

"And René is from the *Italian* side of the family!" Grandmère practically screamed. "He's not even a Renaldo. He's hardly even related to us!"

Luisa looked hurt. "I'm from the Italian side of the family," she said. "And I'm not a Renaldo. Does that mean I'm not related to you?"

"Of course you are, dear," Helen said, patting her on the shoulder, making me feel a bit guilty for thinking, *Sometimes I wish you weren't.* "Princess Clarisse is exaggerating. The Renaldos and Albertos and Ferraris are all very closely related . . . and of course the Italian border is only a mile away from here."

"Well," Dad said, scanning the letter, which Mia had passed to him. "This might explain it. Apparently, Cousin René and his wife paid for one of those home genetic ancestry kits that are so popular right now, and it turns out little Morgan's DNA is ninety-nine-point-nine percent Genovian."

"What difference does *that* make?" Grandmère demanded.

But I knew. Before the words were even out of Dad's mouth, I knew:

"Well," he began. "It means that little Morgan—"

"—doesn't have any *American* blood in him," I said, "like we do."

I tried not to sound as sad as I felt, but it was hard. I knew this whole princess thing was too good to be true.

Not that being a princess is so important. What's important is that, after spending most of my life living with people who never cared for me, I've finally found a family who does. The fact that they're royal—and so am I—has only been frosting on the cake.

Of course, you can learn to get along with unfrosted cake . . . but life with it is so much sweeter.

"Well, not *American* blood, necessarily," Mia said. "But they're claiming that Morgan's DNA is genetically a much closer match to the DNA of Princess

Rosagunde, the founder of Genovia, than either mine or yours, Olivia, because we have American mothers. Which, if you ask me, is simply—"

"*Ridiculous!*" Grandmère cried, rising from her seat. "Who has shown more of Princess Rosagunde's devotion to the crown than either you or your sister? Why, it's because of you, Amelia, that Genovia has one of the highest gross national products in the EU! And you, Olivia, helped keep your school from suffering a humiliating defeat last month in the Royal School Winter Games!"

"Well, I don't know about that," I said modestly. "All I did was take photographs for the school paper."

"But that's certainly more than your cousin René has ever done!" Grandmère insisted. "How dare he imagine he or his son is anything like our noble Rosagunde, whatever some DNA test says?"

"Wait," Nishi whispered. "Who is Princess Rosagunde again?"

"Oh," I said. "She's the one who, in the year AD 568, killed a Visigothic warlord and saved the country from being invaded. Genovia has been ruled by her descendants, the Renaldos, ever since."

"Cool," Nishi said, impressed. Nishi is always impressed by princesses who use weapons and also have extremely long hair like Rapunzel.

"Besides which," Grandmère went on, still on her anti–Cousin René rant, "René is an *Alberto*, so no matter what some DNA test says, neither he nor his child will ever sit upon the throne. There have always been Renaldos on the throne of Genovia!"

"Thank you for that, Mother," Dad said. "It was very *Game of Thrones*. Now, please sit down."

"How could René have even gotten hold of a sample of Rosagunde's DNA to compare with his son's?" Mia asked. "She's buried in a crypt in the royal cemetery."

"Who knows?" Grandmère asked. "Who cares? There's more to ruling a kingdom than simple DNA. One must possess courage, compassion, integrity, intelligence—what qualities, other than his alleged genetic superiority, does this eight-year-old have that make Cousin René think he's fit to rule? *None!* How dare he attempt to stop Amelia's coronation? How *dare* he?!"

"Now, Mother," Dad said. "There's no need to shout."

"How else am I to make myself heard above these shrieking babies?" she demanded. "Where in heaven's name is their nanny?"

"Grandmère," Mia said. "You know we gave the nanny the week off for the holidays—"

Grandmère's face was turning almost as red as Baby Prince Frank's, and he has something called colic.

"The . . . week . . . off . . . for . . . the . . . holidays? Right before the royal coronation?" I thought there was a strong possibility that Grandmère might explode. "Why? Why *on earth* would you do that?"

"Because the poor woman has been working for weeks without a single day off," Mia said, taking Baby Prince Frank from Michael and trying to comfort him. "And it's Christmas. She'll be back by the coronation on New Year's. We can handle this. Or at least . . ." I saw her hesitate a little. "I thought we could before that letter from Prince René."

Grandmère sank into an armchair, clutching the fur collar of her vest. "No nanny," she murmured. "No nanny, and there's a coup afoot! May the good Lord help us all."

"I don't get it," Nishi whispered to me. "How can these people say that you and Mia have no right to the throne just because you're part American?"

"I don't know," I said with a shrug. "But I'm sure it will all turn out okay."

Nishi didn't look convinced, probably because of the scroll on the bottom of the television news station that Dad had just turned on. It said:

ROYAL WRECK!

Apparently, Cousin René had sent a copy of his letter to the press as well as to the palace this morning.

"Aren't you *a little bit* worried?" Nishi whispered to me.

"No," I said. "Not at all."

But I was lying. Of course I'm worried! Especially since a little while ago I overheard Mia saying to Michael, when she didn't know I was listening, "Why does this kind of thing always have to happen right when everything seems to be going great? Why can't I just have a nice, normal family like everybody else?"

Michael said, "Because no one has a nice, normal family. There's drama in everyone's family."

"Not like this," Mia said. "My family seems to have way more drama than anyone else's."

Which is so true! And I know why, too:

Because other people's families don't have thrones—not to mention crowns—over which to fight.

Monday, December 28
8:00 P.M.
Royal Dining Room

Dinner started out super depressing ... and then it got AMAZING.

Depressing because Mia, my dad, and Michael weren't there—they were busy doing stuff with Cousin René's court case, and Helen was busy looking after the babies—which just left me, Nishi, Luisa, Rocky, and Grandmère to eat Chef Bernard's award-winning roasted prawns.

Amazing because of the phone call I got in the middle of one of Grandmère's speeches on the importance of knowing one's royal duty.

"The future princess—or prince—of Genovia has a great many challenges ahead of her," Grandmère was going on, over her prawns. "One of them is to make sure that every citizen of this country feels as if they are part of this community, and that none of the rich culture and heritage of this country is lost or forgotten in an era when most people won't even look up from their screens."

It took me a minute to realize she was saying all this because she'd caught Luisa checking her cell phone under the dinner table—a major etiquette *don't* at the palace dining table!

"Oh," Luisa said, when she noticed Grandmère's death stare. "I do beg your pardon, Your Highness. But I'm expecting an important call."

"Are you, my dear?" Grandmère asked acidly. "From the prime minister?"

"Uh, no," Luisa said, slipping her phone back into her bag. It was a Claudio, of course. Lady Luisa only ever carries Claudios. "My boyfriend, the Duke of Marborough."

"Your boyfriend," Grandmère said. "The duke. How nice. You do realize, don't you, that unless it's an urgent matter of state, phone calls at the table are an abomination?"

"Well," Luisa said snootily, "I doubt Princess Mia actually gets *that* many calls that are urgent matters of state."

This was *not* the right thing to say. Grandmère nearly upset the silver tureen of vegetables (lightly coated with Genovian olive oil) that one of the footmen had been about to pass to her.

"I will have you know, young lady, that there isn't a charity in this country that a member of our family hasn't helped raise awareness of or funds for. The prime minister is *most* indebted to us. The money we generate in tourism alone has kept Genovia's economy afloat for decades. And for centuries the princes and princesses of Genovia have also acted as ambassadors, diplomats, and even warriors for this country, saving it from invasion and ruin time and time again."

Luisa's big blue eyes widened even further than

they had when she'd seen her reflection while wearing the royal crown. "I . . . I'm sorry, Your Highness. Of course I knew that."

"Then why is it," Grandmère asked, "that you told my granddaughter Olivia that it wasn't like Princess Mia would ever actually *do* anything once she's crowned?"

Luisa swung her wide blue stare accusingly at me . . . but all I could do was swallow the mouthful of prawns I'd just taken and shrug.

"What?" I whispered. "I didn't tell her! I swear!"

I hadn't, either.

But I'd always known that Grandmère had hearing like a bat . . . which, by the way, uses echolocation to find its prey.

I would have stuck around to hear Grandmère yell at Lady Luisa some more, except that at that very moment my phone vibrated in my pocket.

When I snuck it out and looked down at the screen (even though of course I knew doing this was *very wrong*), I saw that it was Prince Khalil calling!

"Um," I said, feeling myself blush. "Pardon me, but may I be excused?"

"Retiring for the evening so early, Olivia?" Grandmère looked bemused. "It's not like you to miss dessert."

"Oh no, I'll be right back," I said, already out of my chair. "I have to go to the bathroom. I mean, the toilette."

I felt terrible for lying, but it was for a very good reason. I hadn't spoken to Prince Khalil in seven days (except for a few texts). He'd been in Paris for the holidays, visiting his grandmother. I *had* to take this call!

Grandmère frowned. "Well then, by all means, go," she said, waving her hand. "There's no need to announce your *exact* destination to everyone when leaving the table, you know, my dear."

"Right," I said. "I know. Sorry. Thanks. Bye. I'll be right back—"

I didn't wait to hear what anyone said next . . . although I was fairly certain Rocky giggled, as he always does when anything to do with a biological function is mentioned. I wasn't going to blow this opportunity to speak to Khalil!

That's why I ran down the hall toward the nearest lavatory, then out the French doors and into the Royal Genovian Gardens to press accept and also to write this, because if answering the phone in front of your relatives and best friend is rude, so is writing in your diary!

But what was I supposed to do? Prince Khalil is my boyfriend . . . sort of.

I'm not actually allowed to have a boyfriend because my dad doesn't approve of girls my age dating. I only turned thirteen last month, which is also when Prince Khalil wrote me a letter telling me that he likes me more than any other girl he's ever met.

He didn't say he *loves* me, or anything, and I haven't told him that I love him.

But he is a boy, and he is my friend, and we hang out together a lot, and there is no other boy who I like better, or who makes me feel more tingly when he smiles.

So I guess, technically, he's my boyfriend . . . even

though I'd never call him that, especially in front of him (or my dad, either)!

I don't know what else to call him, though. "Boy-friend" sounds so . . . I don't know. Like something Lady Luisa would say!

And that's fine for her. I just don't know if it's right for me.

Anyway, I should be allowed to answer a call from my friend-who-is-a-boy if I want to (although not at the dinner table, of course. I know that's rude). I've never had a friend-who-is-a-boy before. I seriously have no idea how I of all people got one, especially one as nice and funny and intelligent as Prince Khalil.

I still sort of can't believe it . . .

"Hello?" I said, once I'd gotten to the privacy of the Royal Genovian Gardens.

"Hi, Olivia!" Khalil said. "Sorry if this is a bad time to call. Were you eating?"

"Oh, no," I lied. "No, no, it's cool."

"Great. I just wanted to let you know we're back in Genovia. My parents and I arrived on the seven-thirty train."

"Oh," I said, grinning like an idiot at the sound of his voice. "That's a good train."

That's a good train? What's wrong with me?

"It is. So when can I see you? I missed you!"

I laughed. It was so good to hear his voice. Also good to hear that he'd missed me, because I'd missed him, too . . . more than I liked to think about.

"I can't wait to see you, too," I said.

The thing I like best about Prince Khalil, besides how kind and thoughtful he is, is that he can always make me laugh, even when I'm sad or upset about something, which isn't very often, but does happen sometimes, such as now.

Also, we have a lot in common, since we both want to be scientists when we grow up—Khalil loves herpetology, and I love wildlife illustration—although sadly for both of us, the royal thing might get in the way of our future careers.

Still, I'm third in line to

the throne, and Prince Khalil's country has erupted in a civil war, so there's a strong chance we'll both get to do what we love for a living instead of having to rule.

"I can't do anything right now, though," I said, "because it's kind of late and I've got my friend Nishi and my cousin Lady Luisa staying with me, and, well, uh, I don't know if you've seen the news . . ."

"Yeah," Khalil said. "I did. That thing about your cousin?"

"Yeah, *that*." I tried to laugh airily the way Grand-mère always does when someone expresses concern about something she doesn't want them to think matters, even though it does, like her tattooed eyeliner. "No need to worry about that, though. The palace legal team is handling it."

This wasn't a lie. Michael's sister, Lilly, and all the other lawyers who work for my dad are scrambling to deal with Cousin René's legal filing. I have no idea how, since it sounds to me like he has a pretty good claim.

"Well, that's good," Prince Khalil said. "Still, it's kind of a bummer."

"Yeah," I said. "It is. But maybe we could hang out tomorrow?"

His voice brightened. "That would be great . . . especially because I have a surprise for you from Paris."

"A surprise?" I was shocked. "From Paris? What is it?"

"If I tell you, then it won't be a surprise, will it?"

"No . . . I guess not." A surprise? What could it be? "But—"

He laughed in a mock-evil way. "You'll find out what it is soon enough. See you later, Alligatoridae."

I smiled. "Okay. After a while, Crocodylidae."

Prince Khalil and I always use the correct names for the families of animal species. It's our thing. Some people (such as my cousin Lady Luisa) might not find that romantic, but I do. Science can be very romantic, though not in a mushy way. It is romantic in a hands-on, evidence-based way.

And nothing is as hands-on as a surprise from your boyfriend—or your friend-who-is-a-boy—whatever it might be!

Monday, December 28
11:30 P.M.
Royal Genovian Billiards Room

Well, it's past my bedtime (though it's a school holiday and I have no public events tomorrow, so it doesn't really matter what time I go to bed), but some of my guests don't want to turn in.

Instead they want to stay up and play with my baby niece and nephew.

Which I totally understand—it's fun to play with babies (when those babies don't actually live in your house and you don't have to listen to them cry all the time).

And when you're royal, these are the kinds of things you have to do—sacrifice your own personal happiness for the happiness of your guests and subjects, one of whom includes your snobby cousin Lady Luisa, whom no one, not even her own parents, likes.

Actually, I guess you're supposed to do those kinds of things even when you aren't royal. It's part of what they keep talking about in school—having good character.

But I'm so tired! I just want to curl up in my bed with Snowball and the nice book on the domestication of horses through time that Prince Khalil gave me for Christmas. (I gave him a book on snakes. We agreed that we'd always give each other books as gifts.)

Which is why I can't believe he's bringing me a surprise from Paris. The book on horses was enough!

"They're perfectly lovely, of course," Mia is saying to her friend Tina Hakim Baba, who just arrived from New York for the coronation. "But we do feel a little overwhelmed occasionally. They never sleep at the same time."

She's talking about the babies, of course.

"And when one of them does fall asleep," Michael says, looking a little dazed, "the other wakes up and starts crying. They. Never. Stop. Crying."

"That's normal at this stage in their development," Tina assures him. She's in medical school, so she would know. "The twins are going through their six-week growth spurt. You have to feed them every two to three hours, or they'll get cranky."

"It's an inherited trait, sadly," Grandmère says, taking a sip of her evening cocoa, which I found out the hard way a long time ago by taking a sip isn't really cocoa. "Your father cried for six years straight. That's why I had no choice but to send him to boarding school."

"Thank you for that, Mother," Dad says.

"Well, you turned out well enough," Grandmère says. "In the end."

"Olivia," Nishi whispers, gesturing for me to follow her. "Come here."

I follow her from the billiards room to the palace hallway, wondering what could be going wrong now. Maybe she'd seen Luisa sneak upstairs and stuff the royal crown into her overnight bag.

But I don't see how that could be possible, since I've been watching Luisa all night and she's done nothing but check her cell phone for messages from the duke (still none).

"Olivia, I have an idea," Nishi whispers to me. "What if we were to offer to help out with the babies until the royal nanny comes back? We could make a fortune!"

"You mean babysitting?" I'm confused. "Like for money? But I already babysit all the time." It seemed like every five minutes someone was saying, *Olivia, could you watch the twins for a second?* and the second turned into fifteen minutes and the fifteen minutes turned into half an hour. Not that I minded. I liked having a family who trusted and loved me.

"Sure," Nishi says. "But you're still doing it for free."

"Yes," I say. "Because I'm their aunt. That's what aunts are supposed to do. That, and help sneak their nieces and nephews into horror movies when they're old enough." I know this from watching the Disney Channel.

"But with the nanny gone, and your sister so busy

with this lawsuit thing, we could actually make money watching the babies for her." Nishi looks excited. "We could even offer to babysit all the other little kids of the guests who are going to be showing up for the coronation . . . you know, if there *is* a coronation."

I frown. "Nishi, how can you say that? Of *course* there's going to be a coronation!"

"Then I think this is one of those win-win situations. Your family can obviously use the help, and I for one could really use the money. I don't even get an allowance anymore. My parents cut it off last month. *And* they took away my cell phone."

I'm even more confused. "They did?" I haven't noticed not receiving any texts from Nishi, because she's been visiting, but I ought to have noticed she'd taken zero selfies. "Why?"

She shrugs. "They caught me kissing Dylan. They can't stand him."

"*What?*" I knew Nishi and her new boyfriend, Dylan, had kissed, but she hadn't told me the part about her parents catching her, or not approving of the relationship. "Why don't your parents like Dylan?"

"Shhh," she whispers, since Luisa had overheard my *What?* and was now getting up from her over-stuffed chair by the fireplace and coming to see what we were talking about. Lady Luisa can't stand not knowing everyone else's business. "Dylan was a bit of a bad boy in the past. But it's not a big deal. If you think about it, the Beast, in *Beauty and the Beast*, got in trouble when he was younger, too. But with Beauty's help, he was able to put it all behind him."

"Nishi," I say. "I don't know how to break this to you, since I know how much you love that movie, but *Beauty and the Beast* isn't real. It's a fictional story."

"True," Nishi says. "But every fictional story has a grain of truth in it. And in this case, the truth is that everyone can change. My parents just don't under-stand that. So they cut off my allowance, took away my cell phone, and said I'm not allowed to see Dylan anymore . . . except in school, of course."

"That is so unfair!" cries Luisa. She's shown up in the hallway just in time to hear Nishi's sad story.

"I know, right?" Nishi says. "They almost weren't

going to let me come here to see you, Olivia, except that they thought the separation from Dylan might cause me to forget him—as if that would ever happen!"

"Oh!" Luisa looks outraged. "That's so evil!"

"I know," Nishi says, nodding. "But it won't work. I love Dylan with all my heart."

"Of course you do." Luisa pats Nishi on the arm. "As much as I love Roger." Roger is the name of the 12th Duke of Marborough. It's their family's tradition to name every eldest boy Roger, which almost makes me feel sorry for Roger . . . *almost.*

I can't believe that Lady Luisa and my best friend are bonding over their boyfriends, both of whom seem equally awful.

"What kind of bad things did Dylan do in the past?" I ask Nishi suspiciously. I *want* to think the best of people, like Nishi always does.

But I know from experience—and Nishi should, too—that people don't always have our best intentions at heart. I'm a living example: my aunt and uncle stole all the money my father sent them to take care of me when I was little, and spent it on sports cars and vacations—for *themselves*.

"Oh, you know," Nishi says. "Just normal things kids do. It's all so stupid. Way back in fifth grade he got caught cheating on a test."

I gasp. I can't help it. That's a pretty seriously bad thing to do!

Luisa, on the other hand, rolls her eyes. "Is that all?"

"I know," Nishi says, laughing, too. "My parents are making such a big deal out of it."

"It *is* a big deal," I say. Dylan sounds like a seriously bad boy to me. I've never met him, but I already don't like him, any more than I like Roger the duke. "Cheating? You could get expelled for cheating at the Royal Genovian Academy."

"It was in *the fifth grade*," Nishi reminds me. "It's not like it *mattered*."

"Of course it matters!" I explode. "When you cheat, you're only cheating yourself. You'll never know how well you could have done if you'd only tried!"

Nishi looks even more confused. "Did you read that

on a poster in your guidance counselor's office, or something?"

"Never mind her, Nishi," Luisa says, waving a hand at me dismissively. "She's just jealous because she's never been kissed. Not even by a cheater."

Nishi stares at me. "You and Prince Khalil have never kissed?" I can hardly stand the look of sympathy that appears on her face. "Oh, Olivia! Why didn't you tell me?"

More than ever before in my life, I want to strangle Luisa. But I can't, because I'm her hostess. Instead, I have to be nice to her.

But it's really, really hard.

"My relationship with Prince Khalil is very new," I explain in my most reasonable voice. "It hasn't progressed to kissing yet, and maybe it never will, and that's just fine with me. Everyone matures at their own rate. We don't even like that romantic mushy stuff. And anyway, not everything has to be about physical demonstrations of—"

"Eeeeeeee!" Luisa squeals.

But it isn't because of anything I've said. It's

because her phone has just *ding*ed to indicate that she's gotten a text message. When she looks at the screen, her face is aglow with excitement. "It's *him*!"

"The duke?" Nishi asks, even though it's *totally obvious* from Luisa's joyous expression that it's the duke.

"Yes!" Luisa cries. "It's Roger! And he says he's sorry for not texting me earlier *and* for being such a jerk!"

"That's so great!"

Nishi jumps into Luisa's arms, and the two of them leap around the hallway, hugging each other and screaming as if they've just found out they'd won the lottery. Not even the regular lottery, but the Mega Millions.

Well, I guess the palace walls aren't that thick after all, I want to say sarcastically, but I know they won't hear me. They're too busy having their ridiculous squealfest.

At least until Grandmère comes out and says, "Would you two young ladies *please* keep it down? If your jumping and screaming wakes the royal twins, whom we've *finally* managed to get to sleep, I will hold you personally responsible. We still have a dungeon in this palace, you know, and I have no reservations about sending you there to sleep for the night."

Nishi and Luisa stop screaming and jumping and instead hug all smugly, like they know some kind of secret that I'm not part of, probably about kissing boys.

But that's fine, because I know a secret, too: My dad had the dungeon converted to a wine cellar—and state-of-the-art gym—a long time ago. Tourists still pay eight euros to see it as part of the palace tour (four euros for children, students, and seniors).

Tuesday, December 29
2:00 A.M.
Royal Genovian Bedroom

I'm writing this in my bathroom because Nishi and Luisa are both asleep on air mattresses on my bedroom floor, and I don't want to wake them up by turning on a light to write this. Mostly because that would be rude, but also because then they'll start talking about kissing (and *other things*) that I don't want to hear about anymore.

Of course we have guest rooms with actual beds that they could have slept in, but neither of them wanted to sleep in a guest room because it's much easier for them to torture me from air mattresses on my floor than it is from a guest room.

But I *wish* they'd stayed in their own rooms, because then I wouldn't have had the VERY EMBARRASING MIDNIGHT CONVERSATION that I just had, which I need to write about right now, to get it all out of my head, or I will never, ever get to sleep.

So, yes, it's true:

I'm thirteen years old and I've never been kissed (even though I have a boyfriend. Or at least a friend-who-is-a-boy about whom I feel romantically).

But I don't see what the big deal is! I haven't kissed him yet, either. There's no law that says boys have to kiss girls first. Girls can do the kissing first if they want to.

I just don't want to.

Okay, fine: sometimes I think I want to.

In Europe, you kiss everyone hello and good-bye on both cheeks (usually twice), so technically, I've kissed my friend-who-is-a-boy dozens of times saying hello and good-bye.

But never on the lips.

Really, all we'd have to do to kiss like a proper couple is have one of us move our head slightly while we're kissing good-bye. Just slightly.

And then *BANG*. Khalil's mouth would land on mine, and we'd finally be kissing.

So I guess I know how kissing works. I've seen it done hundreds of times, and I'm not even counting on TV or at the movies. Michael and Mia kiss ALL THE TIME, and so do my dad and my stepmom, and Tina and her boyfriend, Boris P, and even Grandmère and the chief of Genovian security (gross) . . . and don't even get me started on Luisa and the duke. It's crazy, actually, how many people are kissing around me. I can hardly stand it sometimes.

I suppose it's nice that so many people I know are in love.

But I can't help wondering why the person I'm in love with—at least I think I'm in love with him, because the thought of him ever leaving Genovia to go back to his home country, a place I know he longs for, fills my heart with cold, hard terror—doesn't seem to want to kiss me at all.

Maybe he's as nervous about kissing me as I am about kissing him.

"It's true," Nishi said tonight in my room when the subject of kissing came up (she wouldn't let it die after she found out that Khalil and I had never kissed, even though I wanted to drop the subject very much). "Boys are just as nervous about kissing as girls are, even though they try to act cool about it. Dylan told me."

"I really don't want to talk about this," I said from my bed. "I really, really want to talk about something else. Anything else. Anything else at all. Like these." I held up a macaron from the plate beside my bed, which Chef Bernard had given to us as a midnight snack. "Aren't they delicious?"

Macarons are my new favorite dessert. They aren't really cookies, but they aren't really cakes, either. They are two soft little biscuit-y things stuck together with buttercream or jam, and come in assorted flavors. There are ordinary flavors, such as chocolate, orange, vanilla, and raspberry, but then there are weirder flavors and flavor combinations, like pistachio, lychee, rose and passion fruit, and apricot and saffron.

"Yum," I said, popping a chocolate-and-raspberry one into my mouth. "I just love macarons so much."

"Does anyone have a tampon I can borrow?" Luisa asked from her air mattress.

"Oh, I do," Nishi said, and leaned over to grab her toiletry bag.

"Luisa," I said, trying not to sound as exasperated as I felt. "I don't want to talk about *this*, either. And you just had your period two weeks ago. How can you be having it again?"

"Wow, Olivia, I didn't know you kept such careful track of my gynecological functions," Luisa said. "Do you have a special app for that, or something?"

I blushed. "No! I'm just saying that you seem to have your period way more than most people."

"I'm sorry if the fact that I'm so fertile upsets you, Olivia," Luisa said. "I can't help that I'm a woman now and you aren't."

Nishi gasped and sat straight up in bed. "Olivia! You haven't kissed a boy *or* had your period yet?"

Seriously. I'm third in line to the throne of one of the most beautiful countries in the world, and yet this is the kind of thing I have to put up with almost daily in my personal life? I bet this never happened to my sister.

"How could you not tell me?" Nishi demanded. "I thought we told each other everything!"

"I *do* tell you everything, Nishi, except when there's nothing to tell. And how often you have your period has nothing to do with your fertility, Luisa." I could tell by her smile that she was enjoying the fact that she'd upset me. "But if you're really having it as often as you say you are, maybe you should see a doctor, because it's possible you have a tumor, or internal bleeding, or something."

I wasn't trying to be mean, but I've honestly never met anyone who has her period more than Lady Luisa Ferrari. She loves asking people if they have a tampon she can "borrow."

I put "borrow" in quotation marks because sometimes when I hear her ask this, I go, "Gross, Luisa! You're not going to give it back used, are you?" to which she always replies, "Oh, grow up, Olivia. You're so immature."

But if you ask me, *she's* the immature one. The only reason she doesn't carry her own tampons is so that she can ask people if they have one, to show off that she's gotten her period, and that other people (namely me) haven't, to rub it in that it has not happened to them yet.

But that is perfectly normal, according to the Royal Genovian Physician. I asked.

"There is no 'right age' for a girl to get her period," Dr. Khan said. "Whatever is right for her individual body is right. Most girls get it between ages ten and fifteen, with the average being a little over twelve."

So at age thirteen, I'm perfectly normal!

In fact, according to my calculations (based on the number of times Luisa has asked other women—in front of me—if she can "borrow" a tampon), Luisa is the one who is abnormal. She has her period approximately every *three days*, which is a physical impossibility (unless she is suffering from some kind of disorder), since you're only supposed to get it once a month, for approximately four to seven days.

But I happen to know Luisa is *not* suffering from a

disorder, because I made Grandmère ask the baroness if everything was all right with Luisa (you know . . . down there. I know that everything is not all right with Luisa *emotionally*).

And the baroness—Luisa's grandmother—told Grandmère that Luisa is perfectly fine.

And okay, I know it's stupid—and even gross—to get your grandmother involved in a discussion like this. But I felt like I had to do it, because:

a) I was genuinely concerned about Lady Luisa's health.

b) As a future wildlife illustrator, I am interested in biology of all kinds, even human.

c) I had to prove Luisa was faking having her period all the time in order to make me feel inferior for not having had my period at all yet.

Which isn't going to work anymore, because like I said, there is NOTHING WRONG WITH ME!!! To quote Dr. Khan, everyone grows and matures at their own rate.

And no one should be made to feel inferior for not maturing at the same rate as their peers, the way Luisa often tries to make me feel.

"I'm sorry, Olivia," Nishi said. "I didn't know the subject of menstruation was so embarrassing and sensitive for you. If you don't want to talk about it, we don't have to."

"It isn't!" I hissed. "And I'm not embarrassed by it. I'm just saying, Luisa seems to get hers way more than seems normal."

"Do you think that maybe it just *appears* that way to you because you've never had yours?" Luisa asked. "And maybe you're a little jealous because you've never experienced the natural beauty that is menarche?"

"No!" I cried. "And could you not call it that?"

"Why not?" Luisa asked. "As a future wildlife illustrator, I would think you would want to call it by its proper name."

"Menarche *does* sound a little weird," Nishi said. "Let's think up our own code word for it so we can discuss it in front of boys and they won't know what we're talking about."

"Let's not," I said.

"That's a great idea, Nishi," Luisa said. "But what should the code word be? It can't be a normal word."

"'Cake,'" Nishi said. "'Oh, you guys, I got my cake today and I'm so crampy.'"

"That doesn't even make any sense," Luisa said. "We need a better word. How about 'shells'?"

"'Shells'?" I practically yelled. "Why would you do that to the sweet exoskeleton of a marine creature you find by the ocean?"

"I kind of like it," Nishi said. "Like, 'Oh, I got shells, I'm so bloated.'"

"That makes even less sense than 'cake,'" I said. Why was Nishi going along with everything Luisa said? How could she not see how evil and terrible Lady Luisa was? Was this because they'd both kissed boys?

"I love it," Luisa said. "'Shells' it is."

"Great," Nishi said, then held up the tampon she'd found in her bag. "Do you still want this, Lady Luisa?"

"Yes," Luisa said, and snatched it out of Nishi's hand. Then she got out of bed and went to my bathroom, slamming the door behind her, which was rude, because it could have woken the babies, who admittedly are seven doors down in the nursery, but they seem to have inherited Grandmère's extremely sensitive hearing.

"I'm sorry, Olivia," Nishi said softly, after Luisa was gone. "You're not mad at me, are you?"

"No," I said, even though I was, sort of. I didn't know why, though, really. It was good for Nishi to get along with Luisa. Luisa needed *someone* to be on her side, someone who wasn't only doing it to be polite, like I was.

But it still sort of felt like Nishi and Luisa were ganging up on me a little.

"You know, I feel bad; I honestly didn't know how terrible things are going for you here, Olivia" was Nishi's next unexpected comment.

"What?" I said from my bed. "What do you mean? Nothing is terrible for me here."

"Well," Nishi said. "I mean, you do have all these nice things, and you get to live in this great place with a great family and be a princess, and all. But your own cousin is suing you for the crown, and you also have a boyfriend who won't kiss you, and you're thirteen and you still haven't even had your shells yet. So, you know."

Uh, no, Nishi. I don't know. WHY DON'T YOU TELL ME? What am I missing out on, exactly? I'm actually extremely happy and doing great, thanks.

That's what I wanted to say. That's what I wanted to yell, actually.

But I didn't think it would be very polite. So all I said was, "You know, Nishi, we all grow and mature at our own rate."

"Well," Nishi said. "Yes, I know. But—"

"So just because I'm not doing things at the same rate as you and Luisa doesn't mean my life is any better or worse than yours."

"Oh," Nishi said. "Okay. Well . . . I guess that's true."

"Don't *guess* that it's true, Nishi," I said. "It *is* true. There is plenty of empirical data to support it. It is a *fact*."

"Fine," Nishi said. "You don't have to be so defensive about it."

"I'm not," I said. "At least, I'm not trying to be. Sorry."

"I'm sorry, too," Nishi said. "Does this mean we can't try the babysitting thing? Because I really need the money. And I think we'd be good at it. At least you and I would." She lowered her voice to a whisper. "I'm not so sure about Lady Luisa. She's a little bit of a snob."

"Yes," I said, feeling relieved that on this, at least, Nishi and I were still in agreement. "She is. But, I mean, we can try it if you really want to."

"Good. Because even though you can't change the thing about your period," Nishi whispered, "or getting Khalil to kiss you, or the thing with your cousin suing for the crown, you can at least get your dad to pay you for babysitting the twins."

I stared up at my bedroom ceiling. Have I mentioned that there is a mural on it painted to look like the sky, with big fluffy white clouds and pretty birds flying around in it?

Well, there is.

"Fine," I whispered. "We can ask him tomorrow."

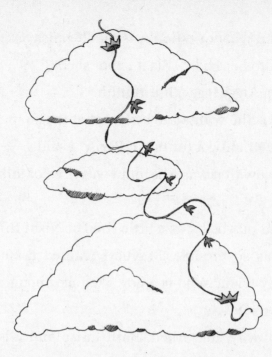

"Whisperers at the table shall breakfast in the sta-
ble," Luisa said as she came flouncing out of the
bathroom. This is one of Grandmère's favorite expres-
sions. It means that people who get caught telling secrets in front of other people will get kicked out of the
house, which is ridiculous, since Luisa doesn't own
this house. My dad and my sister do.

"Ha ha, Luisa," I said. "We aren't even at the table.
Nishi was just asking me a question."

"And what question was that?" Luisa asked, getting back into her bed. "Was it about shells?"

Ugh. Uggggggggghhhhhhhh.

"No. She wanted to know what the surprise is that Prince Khalil got for me in Paris," I said.

I know that was a lie, but I was tired of talking about shells.

And maybe I was a little tired of Nishi thinking my life was so terrible. Maybe I wanted them to know that my friend-who-is-a-boy liked me enough to get me a surprise.

Anyway, it worked. Both Luisa and Nishi stared at me.

"Prince Khalil got you something in Paris?" Luisa asked. There was definitely a note of jealousy in her voice. "What is it?"

"How would I know?" I asked with a shrug. "It's a surprise. He's going to bring it when he comes over."

"What could it be?" Nishi was excited. I could tell because she was hugging her knees to her chest, which she always does when she's sitting down and gets excited. "If it's from Paris, it has to be something really great!"

"Like designer perfume," Luisa said. "Or a new dress by Claudio!"

"Or jewelry!" Nishi cried. "Oh, Olivia, what if it's another diamond heart pendant like you got for your birthday from Prince Gunther? You didn't want a heart necklace from him, but from Prince Khalil, that would actually be romantic. You're so lucky!"

I highly doubt that Prince Khalil got me perfume, a dress by Claudio, or a diamond heart pendant in Paris. For one thing, Prince Khalil knows me pretty well, and knows I'm not interested in any of those things. And for another, Prince Khalil's family was lucky to escape from his country just before it was plunged into civil war, which means they have hardly any money, even though they're royal. He certainly isn't going to spend what little money he has on a silly present for me . . .

. . . Although he did give me an amazing birthday present, a piece of very old, very beautiful artwork from his country.

But I donated that to the Royal Genovian Museum for safekeeping, and also because it was something that needed to be shared with the entire world.

I didn't mention any of this to Nishi or Luisa, though. I'm fine with letting them go on thinking that Prince Khalil got me something superexpensive in Paris.

It's better than them feeling sorry for me because I'm some hasn't-had-her-period-yet weirdo who has to carry her sister's ratty old train at the coronation (if there even is one), and who still hasn't been kissed by her friend-who-is-a-boy.

"I guess we'll have to wait and see," I said.

I felt a little better after that. At least until Luisa asked, "What if it's a kiss?"

"What if what is a kiss?" I asked, confused.

"The surprise. What if what he's bringing you from Paris is a kiss?"

Nishi gasped. "Oh! That would be the most romantic gift of all!"

"Um," I said. "No it wouldn't."

"Why not?" Nishi asked.

"Because," I said firmly. "It just wouldn't."

I couldn't say why I felt this would be the case. I just did. I really, really, *really* hoped Luisa was wrong.

But I had to admit another part of me—a teeny-tiny part—hoped she wasn't.

You see why I've had to stay up so late writing this. I'm really confused. Too many things are happening.

I thought I'd feel better after having written all this down. And I guess I do, a little. Enough to go to sleep, at least.

I hope I still feel better about it tomorrow.

Tuesday, December 29
9:30 A.M.
Royal Genovian Bedroom

By the time my dog, Snowball, licked me awake this morning (as she does every morning, because she pretends not to have been fed and wants to see if I'll give her a second breakfast, which I usually do), Nishi was already awake and working on her plan to earn money by babysitting the royal twins (and whatever other kids she could find around the palace).

"Look, Olivia," she said, showing me a sign she'd drawn up. "Isn't it professional? We can make copies from the printer in your dad's office after breakfast."

ROYAL BABYSITTERS AVAILABLE

Do you want the best for your baby?

Then why not hire a ROYAL?

Many months of experience!

Available 24 hours a day!

We have access to limos, so

we can transport your baby anywhere if an emergency arises

(but there won't be an emergency when you hire a ROYAL).

We speak multiple languages!

We have bodyguards!

We have all the best toys, a pony, and a pool!

We are imaginative and playful!

WE HAVE

GREAT MANNERS AND

COMMUNICATION SKILLS

AND

WE WILL TEACH THEM TO YOUR BABY!

References available

-10 euros per hour-

Contact HRH Princess Olivia via Royal Genovian Press Office

I had to admit the sign was very professional-looking. Still, one thing about it bothered me.

"*Ten euros* an hour?" I'm not sure what the exact exchange rate is right now, but a euro is more than an American dollar. "That seems like a lot."

"That's where you're wrong," Nishi said. "If you keep doing things for free—like babysitting your sister's kids, or carrying her stinky robe—you're just going to keep being taken advantage of. That's what Dylan says, anyway."

The more I heard about Dylan, the less I liked him.

"But those are chores," I said. "Household chores that all kids do. Well, except maybe the robe thing. But even so, do you charge *your* parents ten dollars an hour for the chores *you* do around the house?"

"Well, no," Nishi admitted. "But my family's not Genovian royalty. Plus, they'd kill me if I even suggested it."

"See?" I said. "There you go. I guess Dylan doesn't know everything, does he?"

Nishi bit her lip, looking down at her sign. I

wondered if I'd gone too far and made Nishi mad at me for criticizing her boyfriend. If anyone criticized Khalil to my face, I'd be mad.

But then, Prince Khalil would never cheat on a test, or suggest that I demand ten euros an hour to babysit my baby niece and nephew.

Not that Prince Khalil is perfect. He's not. I'm willing to admit that sometimes he talks a little too much about subjects that don't interest me, such as snakes. Snakes are interesting, but not *that* interesting. Sometimes, in fact, Prince Khalil goes on for so long about snakes that I start wishing we could talk about something else. *Anything* else.

But I would never say this to his face.

And I'm sure I can be a little boring about *my* favorite subject, which is wildlife illustration, and the fact that hand-drawn wildlife illustration is a sadly dying art thanks to computers. Almost everyone draws with computers now.

But I guess Nishi wasn't mad, since she said, "Let's show the sign to your grandmother and see what she

says. I bet she'll think we should go for it! You know how she is about princess warriors and empowering yourself and all that."

I was so relieved that Nishi wasn't mad that I said, "Okay, sure. Why not? We can try."

I'm sure Grandmère is going to disapprove of Nishi's sign and say it's not proper for young royals to go around asking for money for duties they should perform for free out of loyalty to the crown.

But whatever. It can't hurt to try.

"What's going on?" Luisa asked, drowsily lifting her head from her pillow.

"Oh, nothing," I said. "Nishi is going to start a royal babysitting service so she can earn enough money to buy a cell phone since her parents took hers away in punishment for kissing her boyfriend, Dylan, who they don't like."

"A royal babysitting service? That's not a bad idea." Luisa pushed her comforter back. "I could always use a little extra cash."

I was shocked. I'd expected Luisa to laugh at the whole idea. She hates work. At school when we do charitable events, Luisa only signs up because it's mandatory.

And then if you have the bad luck to be assigned to a shift at the same time as her, such as at a bake sale or whatever, she doesn't do anything except sit there and text or watch makeup tutorials on her phone the entire time.

Grandmère says this is another sign of Luisa's lack of character.

"Claudio is coming out with his new line of spring bags, and I don't think my parents or my grandmother understand how much I need all of them," Luisa went on, finger combing her long hair to get rid of her bed head, which of course she only thought she had, because Luisa wakes up looking perfect. "I might as well get used to becoming an independent woman and buying my own."

Oh. So that explains it.

This was one of the most sensible things I'd ever heard Luisa say (even if it was about her favorite fashion designer's handbags. Not that I'm judging. Everyone is entitled to their own hobbies).

Was my good influence finally rubbing off on her, the way Grandmère said it might someday?

I can hardly believe it. It's quite a turnaround from last night. Maybe I misjudged her. Maybe Luisa really *did* have PMS, or something, and now she's feeling better.

I feel kind of bad for suspecting her of faking her period to make me feel insecure.

Tuesday, December 29
10:15 A.M.
Royal Dining Room

We showed Nishi's sign to Grandmère...

And she loved it! She loved it so much that she snatched it out of Nishi's hands and showed it right away to Mia and Michael . . . and they said YES!

I was a little surprised by the whole thing, to be honest. Especially when all Mia said was, "Providing you won't take the babies off palace grounds."

I guess I can understand why she'd be willing—even eager—for us to babysit. In addition to everything she was supposed to be doing today to get ready for the coronation—like go to her final gown fitting and check that the bomb squad has swept for explosives beneath all the manhole covers—she now has to go to an emergency meeting at the Genovian courts to deal with Cousin René and his cease and desist. She looked a little stressed.

"No, Your Highness," Nishi said. "Of course. We would never—"

"We'll stay right here," Luisa said firmly. "Well, not here at the breakfast table, but here at the palace."

"It says you have experience." Michael held up our flyer while also balancing Baby Princess Elizabeth against one shoulder and Baby Prince Frank against the other. "What experience is that?"

"Well, I have little brothers and sisters, Your Highness," Nishi said. "And I've babysat for kids in my neighborhood back in New Jersey. Not quite as young as your kids, but—"

"Obviously I've babysat for little Rocky," Luisa said sweetly. "We hang out so often together."

"Hey!" Rocky objected, lowering a forkful of Belgian

waffles. "I'm not a baby! And you've never once taken care of me."

"Of course I have," Luisa said, still using her fakest voice. "Remember that time we were in the royal pool together, Rocky dear, and you swam into the deep end, and I warned you not to?"

"That never happened," Rocky scoffed. "I'm an excellent swimmer."

"Now, now," said Mia's friend Lana. Like Michael's sister, Lilly, Lana is visiting from New York City for the holidays, and also to see the coronation. She is very tall and stylish. "Let's not ruin such a beautiful morning with silly arguments. I'm more excited than I can say about this babysitting service of yours, Olivia. When does it start? Because little Purple Iris here has just been itching for some playtime with you. You're one of what she likes to call 'the big kids.' Purple Iris loves playing with big kids, don't you, Iris?"

"Paytime!" shouted Lana's daughter, Purple Iris, from her high chair. "Paytime wif de big kids!"

Oh no. I'd forgotten about Purple Iris, whom Lana

(or Mrs. Rockefeller, as Mia had told me she's supposed to be called, except that whenever I call her that, Mrs. Rockefeller always laughs and says, "Oh please, sweetie, call me Lana") had named after Beyoncé's daughter Blue Ivy.

But as far as I can tell, Blue Ivy and Purple Iris don't have anything at all in common, except that they both have superrich parents. Purple Iris is white and blond and the bossiest baby I've ever met, even though she's only sixteen months old. She's already been in three beauty pageants and won first place in all of them, according to her mother.

And boy, does Purple Iris know it!

"I bwush," Purple Iris said, stretching a pudgy little hand holding a baby brush out toward me. "I bwush big kid's hair?"

"Oh," Mrs. Rockefeller cried. "Isn't that cute? She wants to brush your hair, Olivia."

"Um," I said. "Oh yes. So cute. No thank you, Purple Iris. I already brushed my hair this morning."

Purple Iris frowned and banged her brush against the tray of her high chair. "I bwush!" she cried again, this time more loudly.

"She really likes to brush people's hair," Mrs. Rockefeller said, unstrapping Purple Iris from the chair and setting her on the parquet floor. Purple Iris is very advanced for her age, and can already use full sentences . . . sort of.

"It's the craziest thing. Her first word was 'brush.' She's just obsessed with hair." Mrs. Rockefeller swished around her long blond hair. "I have no idea how she got this way."

"Don't you?" Lilly asked sweetly.

"I bwush," Purple Iris yelled, ignoring her mother's hair and pointing at mine. *"I bwush big kid's hair!"*

I smiled at Purple Iris. I could tell the kid was on the brink of having a full-on baby tantrum if I didn't let her brush my hair.

But my hair isn't like hers or her mom's. Theirs is fine and thin and probably benefitted from being brushed a hundred times a day.

My hair is curly and thick, and if you brush it even

a little, it explodes from my head in a big soft cloud. Which isn't a bad look, depending on my outfit and the occasion.

But considering the fact that I'd already carefully braided my hair this morning in anticipation of being around young children, who might try to pull or stick gum in it, loose was not how I wanted to wear it today.

"Olivia, is this something you really want to do?" whispered my stepmother, Helen, with understandable concern, tilting her head in Purple Iris's direction.

"Um," I said, hesitating because even though I definitely did want to help out with the twins, and also help Nishi make some money (even though I didn't approve of Dylan), I definitely did *not* want to get my hair brushed all day by a baby beautician.

"Of course she's sure," Grandmère declared before I could figure out how to reply. "What could go wrong? Especially since I'm going to be around the entire time. I'm the girls' business manager."

"I'm sorry." Mia looked up from her cell phone. She was apparently receiving an important text, probably from the prime minister. "Their what?"

"Business manager," Grandmère said. She'd picked up the flyer, and now she pointed at it. "In addition to supervising, I'll be handling the scheduling, coordinating, arrangement of transportation, and solicitation of payment for these royal babysitters . . . for a percentage, of course."

"Wait," Nishi said. "A percentage? How much of a percentage?"

"Ten percent should be adequate."

"*Ten percent?*" Nishi's voice cracked. "But that's not fair!" Then she added, with a glance at Grandmère, "Begging your pardon, Your Highness."

"You are pardoned," Grandmère said. "I'm a businesswoman. I don't take things personally."

This seemed like kind of an exaggeration. Once the Royal Genovian Yacht Club had to cancel Grandmère's lunch reservation because there was a fire in the kitchen and they'd had to close for the day, and Grandmère wrote a three-page, single-spaced letter of complaint to the local newspaper, which printed it in full.

"You guys." Nishi leaned in to whisper to Luisa and me. "I don't know about this."

"Yeah," I said, glancing over at Purple Iris, who was now waving her brush at Snowball, my dog, and yelling, "I bwush! I bwush!" while Snowball slunk away backward, looking terrified. "Maybe we should start a lemonade stand or something instead."

"I don't know," Luisa said with a shrug. "All the top models and online personalities have managers."

"Yes," I said. "But not *babysitters*."

"*Royal* babysitters, however," Grandmère said, having overheard us—I knew she had hearing like a bat—"have managers, I'm quite sure. And you'll especially need my services when the rest of our guests— visiting royals and foreign dignitaries from all around the world—begin arriving for your sister's coronation. They're all going to want you to look after their children, too."

My eyes widened. I'd forgotten about this. There could be *more* babies like Purple Iris. "But won't they bring their own nannies?" I asked.

"Of course," Grandmère said. "But obviously they'll prefer to hire you. Who wouldn't want a *royal* babysitter caring for their children instead of a commoner?"

"I know I would," Mrs. Rockefeller said. "I want my baby to learn great manners and communication skills, like it says on your flyer. Not that she doesn't have them already." She looked adoringly at Purple Iris, who was now trying to brush Grandmère's poodle, Rommel, even though Rommel didn't have any fur due to an allergic reaction to air. "Aw, that's right, baby," Mrs. Rockefeller said. "Bwush the widdle doggie. Bwush it. Bwush it!"

"Good heavens," Grandmère said, and glared at Nishi. "Don't just stand there. Go and do your job before that child brushes my dog to death."

Nishi's eyes had lit up at the mention of all the other royals who'd be showing up with their babies. "Smartphone!" she whispered excitedly as she rushed over to grab Purple Iris. "I'm going to buy myself my own brand-new smartphone and call Dylan every chance I get!"

I guess she wasn't really thinking ahead about the fact that the whole coronation could be canceled if things went wrong with Mia's meeting with the Genovian judges, and then there'd be no visiting children of royal dignitaries for us to babysit at all.

"Okay," Michael said. "So I guess that's settled." He passed Baby Princess Elizabeth to Luisa, along with the spit-up cloth. That's a white cloth that you wear on your shoulder when you hold a newborn baby so that when she spits up, it won't get all over your clothes. Luisa held it like it might be radioactive. "Olivia's taken care of them before, so she knows their schedule and where everything is . . . like the bottles Mia will make sure to have available throughout the day. Right, Mia?"

"Right." Mia looked up from her phone. A lot of people were calling her, probably over the Cousin René thing. "Sorry. I'll have some for you every two hours. You just let me know where you are. And Olivia, don't forget, you have your dress fitting today, too."

"Yes, of course," I said, taking the baby and the spit-up cloth from Luisa, since she looked like she was about to faint.

"Hey, what about me?" Rocky asked. "Can I be a royal babysitter, too?"

"Of course you can," Nishi said. She was letting Purple Iris brush her long dark hair, which, unlike mine, was not curly. "We're going to need all the help we can get."

Rocky cheered. "Yay!"

"But don't expect a percentage of our earnings," Nishi informed him. "You'll have to work out your own fee."

"Now, hold on a minute," Dad said. He'd taken the flyer from Michael. "Just how many of you am I going to be paying to look after these twins? They're only babies, after all. They don't even walk. It can't take that many people to look after a couple of babies who don't even do anything but sleep, cry, and eat."

"Really?" Helen asked him. "Would you care to take your day off to look after them?"

"Well," Dad said. "No. But—"

"They're *my* babies," Mia said, taking a screaming Prince Frank from Michael. "I'll be the one paying, Dad."

"I don't think the kids are being unreasonable," Helen said, raising her voice to be heard above the little prince's crying. "After all, Frank does require considerable extra care, since he has colic."

Luisa looked pale. "What's colic? I can't be coming down with anything before the coronation—I promised my social media followers I'd post photos. They're all counting on me."

"Colic isn't catching," Tina Hakim Baba assured her. She was sitting at the dining table beside Mrs. Rockefeller, enjoying morning coffee and croissants. "Frank's tummy hurts a little, is all."

"And he farts a lot," Rocky added. Rocky was delighted as always that an opportunity had arisen to use a reference to a biological function in conversation.

"It helps if you hold him and sing," Mia said.

Luisa looked panicky. "Sing what?"

"Oh, anything," Michael said. "But he seems to like classic rock the best. 'Honky Tonk Woman' by the Rolling Stones is his favorite."

"I don't know that song," Luisa said.

"Don't worry," Grandmère said. "I do. Mr. Jagger wrote it about me. But that's neither here nor there.

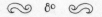

The point is, under my guidance, Genovia's new royal babysitting service is going to do wonderfully."

I really hope Grandmère is right. But somehow I think this whole thing might turn out to be a disaster . . .

Especially after Mia added, "Oh, and one last thing. Cousin René and his wife, Bella, have just arrived from Italy. They're going to need someone to look after Prince Morgan while they're meeting with us. You don't mind babysitting him, do you, Olivia?"

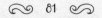

Tuesday, December 29
12:30 P.M.
Royal Pool

Do you want to know the truth? YES. YES, I DO MIND BABYSITTING PRINCE MORGAN. VERY, VERY MUCH.

I understand that he's my cousin (several times removed) and that this morning I volunteered to start a royal babysitting service here in the palace (even though it was all my best friend's idea).

But that doesn't mean I want to babysit the kid of the man who is trying to steal the crown away from my family.

I wasn't the only one, either. Rocky had a lot to say about it, too, when Mia first asked us.

"You're letting Cousin René stay here, even though he's suing us?!" he yelled.

Mia hung up her cell phone.

"Please lower your voice, Rocky," she said very calmly. "You'll wake the babies. And in answer to your question, yes, of course we're allowing Cousin René and his family to stay here. We may be having a disagreement, but we're still family. When you and I have an argument, I don't lock you out of the house, do I?"

I tried to remember when Mia and I had ever had an argument. This may actually have been the first one.

"Of course you wouldn't lock *us* out of the house," I said. "But we live here. Cousin René has his own house. He's only visiting. I really think it might be okay, under the circumstances, not to let him come."

"Well it's too late, since he's already here," Grand-mère said in her loftiest tone. "Cousin René and his wife and son are our invited guests, so as such, we're to treat them with the honor and respect with which we'd treat any guests to the palace, despite their boorish behavior."

"So we have to babysit their son?" I asked.

"Exactly," said Grandmère.

"So they just get *rewarded* for trying to take away your home?" Nishi cried.

"Not at all," Mia said. "By showing them the way they ought to behave, I hope they'll imitate it. It's called modeling."

"Oh, modeling," Luisa said, finger combing some of her long blond hair. "I know all about that. I've been asked to model in numerous local fashion shows to raise money for charity."

"It's not *that* kind of modeling," I said to Luisa. "She means that if we show Prince Morgan kindness, he'll be so impressed he'll want to be like us, and show us kindness in return. Like maybe he'll even ask his father to drop the lawsuit?"

"Something like that," Mia said. "Yes."

I didn't want to tell Mia that I highly doubted her plan was going to work, since you can't change people.

I've been trying for months to make my cousin Luisa a kinder and more thoughtful person, and it's had hardly any effect at all.

But this was something my sister was going to have to learn on her own.

Which is how, a little while later, Rocky, Nishi, Luisa, Baby Purple Iris, and I found ourselves standing outside the door to the guest room Cousin René and his family had been assigned by the majordomo.

"We don't have to babysit this little brat for free, do we?" Nishi whispered to me before we knocked.

"We don't know that he's a little brat," I whispered back. "He could be a perfectly nice kid."

"I sincerely doubt it," Nishi said. "Look what his parents are trying to do to your sister. I think we should tell his dad that our standard rate is *twenty* euros an hour."

"Yeah," Lady Luisa agreed. "It's not like there are any other royal babysitters around that he can hire instead. We've cornered the market."

I lifted my gaze to the ceiling, trying to recall one of the royal lessons I'd learned from Grandmère:

- A smile is your friend—and also your best weapon. Show a friendly face, and your enemy will be so charmed, he'll never know what hit him . . . until later.

"Let's just not mention how much we charge," I said to Nishi as I knocked on the prince's door. "We can simply present him with a bill at the end of the day. If he argues with it, it's Grandmère's problem. She's our business manager."

"Ooooh, you're right," Nishi said with a smile.

The door flew open.

I was interested to see what Cousin René would look like, considering that he and his wife had given birth to such a genetically perfect child as Prince Morgan. In light of what he was doing to us, I thought he should look like a monster.

But when he answered the door, I was surprised to see that he actually looked pretty normal—just like a dad, only, unlike my own dad, not completely bald.

"Babysit Morgan for the day?" he said, when we told him about our offer (leaving out the part about how much we were charging). "How kind of you! I'm sure Morgan would be delighted to spend the day with his little cousins." He glanced at a sullen-looking blond boy slouched in a chair in the corner, playing video games on his smartphone. "Wouldn't you, Morgan?"

"No," Prince Morgan said, after giving us a dismissive stare and returning to his phone.

I was surprised he even had a smartphone. He was only eight. Most kids I knew didn't get them until they were in middle school.

Then again, this kid was a prince.

And he wasn't even that good-looking of a prince, for someone who was supposed to be so perfect. Oh, he had Princess Rosagunde's blue eyes and blond hair, all right.

But other than that, he just looked normal, like his dad, except that he was wearing a suit, slightly formal attire for an eight-year-old. Then again, he was a royal.

"Morgan," Cousin René said in a

warning voice. "Remember what we talked about last night before we came here?"

"No," the prince said, even more rudely, still not looking up from his phone.

Instead of screaming *I believe you mean "No, Your Highness,"* the way Grandmère would have done, Cousin René only sighed. He said, "Of course you remember. About how as the new prince of Genovia, you're going to have to be polite to everyone?"

Him? Prince of Genovia? Ha! If that kid is the prince of Genovia, then I'm a kangaroo.

But I guess Prince Morgan remembered the talk, since he heaved an enormous sigh, then slid out of the chair.

"Fine," he said, coming to the door. "What is there to do around here, anyway?"

"Well," I said. Prince Morgan's fingers were still flying over the keys of his phone. I wondered if he ever put it down. "I have a pony. Would you like to go meet her? I'll let you ride her, if you want."

"Ugh." Prince Morgan actually looked up from his phone and made a face. "I hate animals, especially horses. They're so smelly and dirty. When I become prince, the first thing I'm going to do is rid this palace of all animals."

I almost kicked him in the shins for this—almost. I restrained myself at the last minute, remembering another one of Grandmère's princess lessons:

- A royal does not kick a guest in the shins, or anywhere else, for that matter, unless she is defending herself from bodily harm.

But rid the palace of all animals? Was he nuts? What about Carlos, my pet iguana, who lived in the orange tree in the royal gardens beneath my bedroom window? Maybe I should introduce Prince Morgan to him, so he wouldn't be so prejudiced against animals. I could understand not liking ponies and dogs—some people are allergic to pet dander—but iguanas? They don't even have fur!

What had Carlos ever done to Prince Morgan?

Fortunately, Lady Luisa must have seen the rage in my face, since she stepped in front of me and asked

Prince Morgan, in a voice dripping with sugary sweetness, "What about the pool, Your Highness? You like to swim, don't you? Everyone loves a heated pool, especially one with a slide, in wintertime."

"A pool?" Prince Morgan actually looked interested. I wasn't sure if this was because Luisa's so pretty—even an eight-year-old who was addicted to his cell phone was bound to notice—or because he truly enjoyed water sports. "This dump has a pool?"

"Oh yes," Lady Luisa said. "With views of the beach and the royal garden. One of the perks of being a guest of the Genovian royal family is free twenty-four-hour use of the palace pool."

"Well," Prince Morgan said with a worldly sigh. "I'm not really a guest, since I'll soon own this place, but I might as well see the pool."

Which is why we're here now, with the babies (the twins are both in shaded bassinets, and we're keeping a close eye on Purple Iris to make sure she doesn't drown. She's wearing two sets of arm floaties and a swim vest, and is inside an inflatable inner tube).

Prince Morgan was only interested in the pool for

about five minutes, though. After he went down the slide twice, he said it was "boring" and "had too many steps in the ladder."

Now he's sitting on a lounge chair playing with his phone again, not speaking to anyone except Serena, my Genovian bodyguard, whom he ordered to bring him a butterscotch sundae . . . not realizing until Serena told him that Genovian guards are not waiters, and that bringing little princes butterscotch sundaes is not part of their job description.

Ouch!

I guess Prince Morgan is finding out—like me— that being the heir to the throne isn't the easiest thing in the world after all . . . especially a throne you're trying to steal.

Tuesday, December 29
1:30 P.M.
Still at the Royal Pool

Prince Khalil just texted. He wants to know if now would be a good time to come over. NOW, when I've got a lunatic toddler trying to brush my hair, one royal baby who won't stop crying, who then makes his twin sister start crying, and a little prince who won't stop complaining about *everything*.

Nothing here is as good as it is back at Prince Morgan's villa in Italy, where, it turns out, he has his own private tutors, a miniature Mercedes golf cart that he's allowed to drive into town whenever he wants (can this be true? I don't believe it), and where he's also allowed to eat all the butterscotch sundaes he wants, whenever he wants (I'm definitely sure this isn't true. If it was, he'd be too heavy for his golf cart to move).

I don't think I'm cut out to be a babysitter. Maybe a pet sitter. But definitely not a babysitter.

I don't even know what to say to Prince Khalil. I can't let him come over and witness the madness that is our royal babysitting service. I don't even have any idea when it's going to end. According to Mia, they're still trapped at the Genovian courts. She just sent over more bottles for the babies (not that it does any good. Baby Prince Frank won't take his. All he does is cry).

I am never having children. NEVER EVER EVER EVER.

"I think maybe Baby Prince Frank is sick," Lady Luisa keeps saying.

"Of course he's sick," I said. "We told you. He's got colic."

"Well, maybe we should call Princess Mia and tell her that she needs to come back."

"No!" Nishi really wants her ten euros per hour.

"Colic's not a real sickness. I mean, it is, but it isn't something we can't handle on our own."

"What I believe Miss Desai is trying to say is that a lot of babies get it," Grandmère explained. She's helping to supervise in her capacity as manager of our business. "With proper care, it passes in a few weeks, usually. You simply have to be patient. Rock him with more vigor, Olivia."

I was already rocking Baby Prince Frank pretty hard, but I tried rocking him harder. This only made him hiccup as he cried.

"Hmmm," Grandmère said, taking a sip of her drink. "Curious. That used to work with your father."

"Let me try," Prince Morgan said, miraculously setting down his cell phone for a change. "I'll rock him real hard!"

"That will not be necessary, Your Highness," Grandmère said briskly. "It is not the force of the rocking, but the sentiment behind it. Let me try singing that song that Prince Michael suggested."

Grandmère tried singing "Honky Tonk Woman," but either she didn't know the right words, or Michael was wrong about that being Baby Prince Frank's favorite song, because all Grandmère's singing did was make him cry harder. It made me want to cry a little, too.

Purple Iris tried to help, though: "I bwush?" she asked, waddling toward a screaming Baby Prince Frank's cradle with her hairbrush.

"No!" we all shouted, so loudly that Purple Iris jumped, looking as if *she* might start crying next.

"No, *thank you*," I said to her quickly, remembering that we were supposed to be teaching manners and communication skills to our young charges. "I know you're only trying to be helpful, Purple Iris, but Baby Prince Frank doesn't have very much hair. See?" I pointed to the baby's bald head. "You can't brush what isn't there. It might hurt him."

"No hurt," Purple Iris said, with a trembling lower lip, holding up her brush. "I bwush. I pay wif big kids!"

Oh good grief.

"Why don't you go brush the doggie some more?" I said, pointing at Snowball. "She likes it."

I felt a little bad for lying—Snowball definitely didn't like it—but what else could I do?

Purple Iris beamed. "Okay. Okay, I bwush it." She toddled toward Snowball, who looked panicky and ran away. But that was okay, because Purple Iris waddled so slowly, I knew she'd never catch up. Maybe she'd get tired and need a nap.

"Try a different song," Rocky said. He began to sing "Let It Go" from Disney's *Frozen*.

"No, not *that* song," Grandmère said emphatically, though the song seemed to work. Baby Prince Frank's eyelids were drooping. Grandmère had grown to dislike that song when Rocky and I played it one too many times after Lilly gave us a karaoke machine for Hanukkah. "I believe many babies like sentimental love ballads. Do you know any?"

Luisa held up her phone. "I have an idea. I'll call my cousin Victorine and get her to come over. She's been posting a ton of lip-synchs of herself doing love ballads by Boris P, in preparation for him coming here to perform after the coronation."

"Boris P is coming here?" Prince Morgan suddenly looked less bored.

"Yes," Nishi said. "The international pop sensation Boris P is engaged to Princess Mia's friend Tina Hakim Baba, so she can get him to come to Genovia and perform for free anytime she wants. Of course," Nishi added, looking sly, "he probably won't come anymore if *you* become prince, because he's not personal friends with you."

Prince Morgan stuck out his chin. "He'll come if I pay him to. My father is extremely wealthy. Much wealthier than yours!"

"Well, that wouldn't take much," Nishi said. "I'm only the royal babysitter, not royal myself."

"Hasn't anyone ever told you that it's vulgar to brag about your wealth, young man?" Grandmère asked, eyeing the prince distastefully.

"No," Prince Morgan said. "What is wrong with your eyebrows?"

Before Grandmère could explode with rage—I could tell she was going to, because she prides herself

on how well she draws on her eyebrows—I asked loudly, "What did Victorine say, Lady Luisa?"

"She's coming right over." Luisa looked up from her cell phone. "Of course, she's bringing Marguerite . . . you know the two of them are inseparable."

I did know that. Victorine and Marguerite are cousins, but also best friends.

But they're also MY cousins, so it wouldn't be inappropriate to have them over to the palace while I was babysitting the royal twins, who are basically their cousins, too.

I was so relieved at the idea of anyone being able to stop the crying, I said, "That's great."

"Okay," Luisa said. "But you know what's going to happen . . . they're going to want to invite Prince Gunther, since he's in town with his parents for the coronation, and the three of them have been hanging out nonstop with Princess Komiko and Nadia. Is it going to be all right if all of them come over?"

"Are you kidding?" Nishi cried. "It'd be *great*! I mean, the more help we can get, the easier this will be, right?"

Grandmère looked pleased. "Spoken like a true businesswoman."

I didn't think it was so great, though. "Wait a minute," I said. "What exactly is going on? That's a lot of people. I don't know if we should really be having *that* many people here when we're supposed to be looking after—"

"Oh, look!" Luisa squealed. "The duke just texted! He's wondering what I'm up to."

Nishi clapped. "Yay! He can come over, too."

Luisa choked. "The duke? Help babysit? No way!"

"Why not?" Nishi asked, looking genuinely curious.

"Well, because . . . because . . ." Luisa seemed to be having trouble finding her words. "Roger wants me to come over and play tennis at his house. None of you will mind if I do, will you? Not now that you have so many other people coming to help."

Now I understood what Luisa had been up to, inviting everyone over. It was so that she could go to the duke's house without feeling guilty.

"What I understand," Grandmère said coldly, "is

that you made a commitment to this business and to your friends, and you will honor it."

Luisa looked horrified. "What? No I didn't."

"Pardon me," Grandmère said. "But yes you did. When one agrees to take part in a business, one agrees to stick it out through the good times and the bad. That means one cannot flit off to play tennis with the Duke of Marborough just because one of the babies won't stop crying and another has a very stinky diaper." She pointed at Baby Princess Elizabeth and made a face. "That shows a lack of both character and work ethic."

"Yes," I said. "And I thought you wanted to become an independent woman, Luisa, so you could buy your own Claudio handbags."

"I do," Luisa said with a sniff. "But that was before I knew working was so hard."

"Of course work is hard," Grandmère said. "That's why they call it work. If it were easy, they'd call it something else . . . like happy fun playtime."

Rocky laughed. "Happy fun playtime! I like that."

"Paytime!" Purple Iris echoed. "I pay wif big kids?"

"Work is nearly always difficult and just as nearly always unpleasant," Grandmère went on, ignoring them. "But one does it in order to help pay the bills and keep the world an orderly place, and also to find a sense of personal fulfillment—something Princess Amelia knows, and which is the reason she will make the best ruler of Genovia, not that selfish little beast over there."

"Hey!" Prince Morgan said, looking up from his phone. "I can hear you. And I'm not selfish. My dad says I'm just assertive because I know my own worth."

Grandmère ignored him. "So, contrary to what you might think, Luisa, you have made a commitment, and are not abandoning it to go and play tennis with the duke. Though of course he is welcome to come here and help us babysit."

"Fine," Luisa said grumpily, and whipped out her phone. "I'll tell him. But if that's how it's going to be, then you have to ask Prince Khalil to come over and help, too, Olivia. I don't see why *my* boyfriend should be the only one to have to learn how to change a stinky diaper today."

"Fine," I said. "I will."

And I picked up my phone and texted Prince Khalil, pretending like it was no big deal at all, when it's actually quite a big deal. I don't want my friend-who-is-a-boy to have to endure my hideous relative, Prince Morgan.

But now I guess I have no choice:

OlivGrace **>**

> Hi, Khalil! So, it's fine if you come over, but I'm just warning you that I'm stuck at the palace babysitting my niece and nephew and these other little kids who are visiting. I don't know if you'd be interested in coming over to help, but I just wanted to let you know you can if you want.

Please say no, I prayed. Please say you can't because you're busy. DO NOT COME OVER HERE.

It's not that I don't want to see Prince Khalil.

It's that I don't want to see him in front of Luisa and Nishi now that they'd mentioned the thing about him giving me a kiss as my surprise—even though of course I still don't believe that's what the surprise is.

To my disappointment, however, Prince Khalil texted back mere seconds later:

< PrinceKhalil

> Great! I'll be right over! I've never babysat before, but how hard can it be? Sounds like fun!

Oh no. He has no idea. Should I warn him?

Too late, though, because a few seconds after that, he texted:

> I'm on my way.

> I won't bring your surprise, though. I don't want to give it to you in front of other people. ;-)

He'd mentioned the surprise!!!! So it couldn't be a kiss, if it was something he had to "bring," like in a gift bag, or something.

Luisa had a different idea, though.

"Oh, your surprise!" she cried. Like an idiot, I wasn't holding my phone tightly enough, so Luisa was able to snatch it away and read Khalil's messages. "It must be a kiss after all!"

She managed to say this right in front of my grandmother!

Thanks, Luisa.

"What?" I cried, blushing. "No it isn't. Look, he said he wasn't going to *bring* it. You don't *bring* a kiss."

"Sure you do," Luisa said. "He only said that to throw you off. It's totally a kiss. A great big one!"

Grandmère handled the whole thing pretty calmly, though. She said, "It would be quite nice of the prince to give you a kiss as a gift, Olivia. A kiss in the new year always brings good luck. Now, really, children: this baby is smelling as ripe as a Genovian orange left too long in the sun." She pointed at Baby Princess Elizabeth. "Whose turn is it to change this baby's diaper?"

"I believe it's yours, Your Highness," Luisa said sweetly to Grandmère, completely forgetting to torture me over Prince Khalil and his surprise gift.

"Oh no," Grandmère said just as sweetly back to her. "I'm management. Management does not change diapers."

"Well, I'm not doing it," Luisa said. "I'm only a cousin. Cousins don't change diapers. That's something aunties do!"

So that's how I changed the first of many dirty diapers for the day!

Grandmère is right: work is definitely called work—and NOT happy fun playtime—for a reason!

Tuesday, December 29
3:30 P.M.
Royal Pool

I was right about the day turning out to be a disaster. Luisa has invited over our whole class, practically.

Well, okay, maybe not our whole class.

But definitely the duke and all his friends, none of whom are interested in taking care of babies.

Even worse, they all got here at the same moment as Prince Khalil, so my first time saying hello to him again after being separated for a whole seven days was extremely awkward! There were all these people watching, and I don't even mean people like the majordomo. But also people like Luisa and my grand-mother.

So when Prince Khalil walked in, I had to act cool, even though my heart skipped a beat at the sight of him (cheesy as that sounds). He just looked so good! Especially because he was smiling so wide at seeing me (at least, I hope that was why).

"Hello, Princess Olivia," he said, coming over to take my hand to shake it. (We had to be very formal, because of Grandmère and Prince Morgan and the majordomo and all.) "It's nice to see you again."

"Why, hello, Prince Khalil," I said, just as formally. "It's nice to see you, too."

Meanwhile, I was smiling so hard, I thought my cheeks would burst in two . . . especially when he leaned down (he is slightly taller than me) and kissed me.

Only on the cheek, of course! First one cheek, then the other. This is the standard greeting in Genovia. My surprise gift DEFINITELY wasn't a kiss . . . at least, not the kind Luisa and Nishi meant!

Then, just as he pulled away, and I was gazing into his dark eyes, wondering if Luisa was right, and my surprise really was a kiss, only maybe coming at a different time, the duke yelled, "Cannonball!" and ran past us and jumped into the pool, making such an enormous splash that both of us got wet.

"It's fine," Luisa said, when I went up to her to complain about her boyfriend's behavior. "Babies like excitement."

But I don't think babies like dukes doing cannonballs in the pool right next to them (and by babies I do not mean me and Prince Khalil, I mean my niece and nephew).

Well, not *next* to them, exactly—I would never let that happen. But close enough that several drops of water landed on Baby Princess Elizabeth's tiny cheek, despite the cover over her royal bassinet.

"Luisa," I said through gritted teeth, when the duke

got out of the water and walked over to the diving board to try another jump. "This is inappropriate."

"Oh, Stick," Luisa said with a laugh. "You worry too much."

Stick is the nickname Luisa calls me when she thinks I'm acting like a stick-in-the-mud.

"I thought we'd both agreed you were going to stop calling me Stick," I hissed. I was aware that Prince Khalil was watching us curiously.

"I would if you'd stop acting like one. By the way, do you have a tampon I could borrow?"

She said this right in front of Prince Gunther and Victorine and Marguerite and everyone, including Prince Khalil!!! And after the discussion we'd had last night in my room, and our agreement to use the code word "shells," and everything!

"Oh, I do," Marguerite said, and reached into her pool bag.

"I do, too," Nadia said, and reached into hers, as well.

Every girl in my entire class has had their period except me!

Actually, this is not true. I know Nadia has not had hers, because we discussed it once. She only carries around tampons for when she eventually does, and also because Luisa is always asking for them. Nadia says she feels sorry for Luisa, "because her grandmother doesn't remember to buy her personal hygiene supplies!"

Ha! That's not the reason Luisa is always asking for tampons.

Prince Khalil—and all the rest of the boys, including Prince Gunther—was too polite to mention the incident, if he'd even noticed. I'm not sure he couldn't have, though, really.

But it doesn't matter, because after that we were too busy anyway with Purple Iris, who was delirious with joy over the fact that all these new people had arrived.

"I bwush?" she kept going up to boys like the duke and asking, holding out her pudgy little fist, her baby brush clutched tightly in it, while pointing to his hair. "I bwush?"

"What?" the duke said, dodging to get away from her. "No way!"

"Aw, come on," Prince Khalil said. "Have some pity for the poor kid."

"Your funeral, Leel," the duke said, laughing. Leel is the nickname the duke and some of the other boys call Khalil, which is pronounced *Kuh-LEEL*.

Prince Khalil ignored him. "You can brush my hair, little girl," he said to Purple Iris, and sat down on a chaise longue so Purple Iris could reach his hair to brush it.

Although I think he soon regretted it, because Iris was not the gentlest of hairstylists.

"Ow," Prince Khalil said. "Um, could you not— Whoa, this kid is strong."

"Oh my gosh, that is so adorable," Marguerite said, snapping a photo of Prince Khalil getting his hair brushed by Purple Iris.

"I know," Nadia said, snapping a photo of her own. "I'm so posting this."

The one good thing about Luisa calling all my friends and having them show up while we were trying to babysit is that she was right about Victorine: she did know all the words to every Boris P song, and Baby

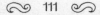

Prince Frank loved them all! He actually stopped crying when she sang them . . .

But only Boris P songs, and only when *she* sang them . . . He would burst out crying again if anyone else tried to sing.

At first Victorine seemed pleased and flattered by this.

But after about the eighth song, she began to look a little scared.

"You guys," she whispered over the top of Baby Prince Frank's head. "I'm going to have to sit here and do this all day? Is this kid ever going to fall asleep?"

"No," Rocky said. "But at least he's not crying. Oh wait—"

Baby Prince Frank had begun to cry because Victorine wasn't singing. She hastily began singing again.

"Seriously," she sang, as if her words were part of the song. "My throat is starting to get dry."

"Tea," cried Grandmère, clapping her hands—but not loudly enough to wake Baby Princess Elizabeth, who'd finally fallen asleep now that her brother wasn't crying and keeping her awake. "I'll order some hot tea with honey from the kitchens right away in order to soothe your vocal cords. We must do all we can to keep them relaxed, particularly up until and during the coronation. You've become a vital asset to our team, young lady! We cannot lose you. It's essential that we keep that baby quiet while his mother is being crowned."

"You mean *if* she's crowned," Prince Morgan said with a sniff. "Who'd allow babies in a throne room? Loud, nasty things!"

"Not allow the babies to attend their own mother's coronation?" Grandmère shook her head. "That would be an abomination! When they grow old enough and realize they were purposefully excluded from one of the most important days in Genovian history, they'd very rightly never forgive us!"

Prince Morgan rolled his eyes. "They could always watch it later when they're older, on video."

"Watch it on video?" Grandmère looked as outraged as if he'd suggested she wear an evening gown to brunch. "Knowing one has attended something live, young man, even when one is only a few weeks old, is always superior to watching it on a screen. Always!"

I couldn't believe we were even talking about this, given that, depending on the outcome of the meetings my sister was having, there might not even be a coronation. But whatever.

I now have more important things to worry about, such as the fact that Serena, my bodyguard, has just reminded me about my dress fitting.

"Your Highness, have you forgotten?" She looked a little irritated by all the splashing—mainly from the water polo game that Prince Gunther had started—and probably by the fact that Prince Morgan continued to forget she's not a servant, and kept asking her to get him things from his room or the palace kitchen, like his sunglasses or a Coke. "Your gown for the coronation. Your fitting is right now."

I totally forgot!

This is the kind of thing that slips your mind when you're surrounded by babies and young royals who are having an impromptu pool party instead of doing what they're supposed to be doing, which is babysitting.

"Uh," I said, turning to Prince Khalil, who was still bravely allowing Purple Iris to brush out his curls.

"I'm sorry, Khalil. But I have an urgent matter of state to attend to. I promise I'll be back just as soon as I can, but in the meantime, do you think you can keep an eye on things around here while I'm gone? I'd ask Nishi, but . . ."

Nishi couldn't seem to take her gaze off a shirtless Prince Gunther, who was playing goalkeeper. *Nishi, who keeps telling me how much she misses Dylan, and who is supposed to be babysitting!*

Prince Khalil smiled, even though I was certain what Purple Iris was doing to him had to be a little uncomfortable. His hair was standing at least three inches on end.

"Of course," he said. "And maybe later, when you're finished babysitting, you and I could go get an ice cream or something?"

I smiled back, my heart thumping happily the way it always does when he suggests going to get an ice cream. That's the special thing we'd done on our first ever . . . well, not *date*, since we're not *dating*. But the first time we ever admitted to having a special liking for each other, we'd sat on the seawall in downtown

Genovia, eating ice cream and gazing out at the ocean while almost but not quite holding hands.

"I would *love* that," I said, even though I couldn't see how it was ever going to happen with all this craziness around us, plus my royal duties.

I hated to leave him here in the clutches of Purple Iris, the terrifying baby hairstylist, but what else could I do? One time I was late to a royal fitting, and Sebastiano, left to his own devices, sewed gigantic orange elephants all over the dress he had designed for me. He said he felt the elephants showed the true me, "a young and inno girl." (He meant "innocent." Sebastiano doesn't speak English very well.)

When I asked him (very politely) to please remove the elephants because I'm not seven years old, he got very insulted.

Artists, particularly fashion designers, can be extremely temperamental. Grandmère says you have to handle them with kid gloves or they'll just go all to pieces, and then they're of no use to anyone.

Tuesday, December 29
4:45 P.M.
High Tea
Royal Genovian Gardens

I'm not going to say that today was the worst day ever, because I've definitely had worse. There was that day back at my old school in New Jersey when Annabelle Jenkins punched me in the face for no reason. (Well, it turned out there was a reason, but not a reason that made sense to anyone but Annabelle Jenkins.)

That was worse.

Today was close, however. No one punched me in the face, but having to babysit one toddler, twin infants, a spoiled little prince, AND Lady Luisa felt a lot like getting punched in the face.

Especially the Lady Luisa part. I've always known she had problems. Why else would she constantly tell me I'm immature and ask me all the time if she can borrow a tampon when she knows I don't have one? That is not the behavior of a self-loving individual. I've always known that that is the behavior of a person with issues.

But what I did not know was that she was completely and totally irresponsible and also possibly a criminal.

But I sure found out today, when I came back from my gown fitting.

Sebastiano has really outdone himself this time. No orange elephants. The dress he's made for me is of pure cream-colored silk, cinched in at the waist with a full ball-gown skirt and tiny off-the-shoulder puffed sleeves, so light and airy that I don't just look like a princess in it: I look like a fairy princess, but one of those cool ones who cast spells.

I found everyone sitting in an exhausted heap

around the pool . . . everyone except for Luisa and the duke.

Prince Gunther's game of water polo had apparently tired out even the Marquis of Tottingham, who's been known to go for thirty-six hours without sleeping, thanks to the number of energy drinks he regularly consumes, even though Mia says those are quite bad for children.

"Where are Luisa and the duke?" I asked.

Nishi lifted a drowsy head. Amazingly, Baby Prince Frank was dozing happily in her arms, having finally been lulled to sleep by a now completely hoarse Victorine.

"I saw them going into the palace a little while ago," Nishi said. "I think they said they were hungry and were going to get a snack."

The day Lady Luisa Ferrari says she's hungry is the day I'll join the Stockerdörfl ski team. She's been on a diet since she was six years old, thanks to unhealthy body images she's picked up from all her grandmother's European fashion magazines.

"I believe Lady Luisa and the duke may have gotten

lost on their way to the kitchens," Grandmère said, as she burped a recently fed Baby Princess Elizabeth. "Perhaps you and Prince Khalil ought to go look for them, Olivia, and help them find their way back here."

Prince Khalil and I were only too happy to do so, since this meant we finally got a little alone time together.

We just never expected to find Luisa and the duke doing . . . well, what they were doing.

As we searched—first in the kitchens, where there was no sign of Luisa and the duke: Chef Bernard said he hadn't seen them—Prince Khalil asked how my dress fitting had gone, and I told him. Then I asked how Paris had been, and he told me. Then I asked how things were going in his native country. It had been a while since we'd had a chance to talk alone together in person, so it was nice to catch up.

Things weren't going so well in his native country since his uncle had taken it over in a military coup and Khalil and his family had been forced to flee. But he likes living in Genovia—even though he hopes to go back someday, if his uncle can be dethroned.

"Being a royal is complicated," I observed, as we searched in the Hall of Portraits for Luisa and the duke.

"It really is," Khalil agreed.

"I mean," I said, "I guess my family could turn out like yours if the courts rule that Prince Morgan is the true heir."

"Well," Khalil said. "Not really. What happened in my country would only happen in yours if Prince Morgan's dad has an army and tries to take the throne by force."

I thought about that. "You're right. That would never happen in Genovia. Mia would immediately step aside. She'd be too worried about people getting hurt not to."

Khalil nodded, his adorably thick eyebrows slanted down into a troubled frown. "Exactly."

I realized I probably shouldn't have brought it up, since the whole thing made Khalil look sad. "Hey," I said, reaching out to take his hand. "Do you know what Rocky and I like to do sometimes?"

He looked at me bewilderedly. "No. What?"

So I told him how Rocky and I like to slide down the

Hall of Portraits in our socks, then asked if he wanted to try . . .

I knew that my cousin Luisa would say I was being hopelessly immature. Thirteen-year-olds do *not* spend their recreational time sliding up and down hallways, particularly in palaces.

But Prince Khalil's dark eyes lit up, exactly the way I'd hoped they would. "Yes, please!"

So we tried it.

But of course it didn't work, because we didn't have socks on. We were wearing sandals, since we'd been at the pool. And everyone knows you can't slide on floors while barefoot: the bottoms of your feet stick to the parquet.

"Wait," I said finally, nearly breathless from all the laughing we'd been doing, watching each other getting a running start, then attempting to slide. It had been so funny, and the perfect antidote to his depression over his family situation. His eyes were no longer sad. They were bright with joy . . .

. . . And maybe a little something else. I don't know what, but I liked it!

"Let's run upstairs and get some socks from my room," I said. "We'll be able to slide much better then."

"I thought we were on a mission to find your cousin and the Duke of Marborough," he said with a smile, still with that strange look in his eye. "And what about the Royal Babysitting Service? We're shirking our duty."

"Oh, it will be okay," I said. "I think the Royal Babysitting Service can spare us for a few more minutes."

I took his hand again—his fingers felt so electric and alive in mine!—and pulled him up the Grand Royal Staircase after me, still breathless from all the laughing. He was laughing, too. It was a good thing there weren't any public tours of the palace going on just then (the palace is closed to the public for the holidays), or the tourists would have seen Princess Olivia laughing her head off like a crazy person, running up the Grand Royal Staircase with the Prince of Qalif behind her.

It wasn't until we got to the top of the stairs and turned the corner to the royal apartments that I realized something was wrong.

During the day, when we royals are out and about, the doors to our private bedrooms are left open so that the staff knows that it's all right to go in and make the beds or replenish the fruit bowls or hang the dry cleaning in the closets or whatever it is that needs to be done.

The only time the bedroom doors are closed is when a royal is inside his or her room.

When Prince Khalil and I reached the top of the Grand Royal Staircase, I saw right away that the door to the bedroom that Princess Mia and Prince Michael share was closed.

But that made no sense, because they were still at the courts. If they'd come home, I'd have heard about it, because first of all the majordomo would have announced it, and second of all, the first place Mia and Michael would have gone was the pool, to pick up the twins and give them kisses. That's the kind of parents they are. They're not the kind of parents who would come home and shut themselves up in their room. They *love* their babies. They can't get enough of them, even if they jokingly complain sometimes about all the crying and the pooping.

So why was their bedroom door closed?

"Hold on a second," I said to Prince Khalil, dropping his hand as I started toward the closed door of my sister's room.

"Is everything all right?" Khalil asked.

"I'm not sure," I said.

I walked up to the closed door and laid my ear against it.

I know it's wrong to eavesdrop, but when you live in a palace, it's sort of necessary. Grandmère told me that

many monarchies have been saved by a little well-placed snooping, and that this is why the Throne of England employs James Bond.

But one shouldn't feel reluctant to do a little snooping oneself when the situation arises, so long as one can keep from getting caught.

Through Mia's door, I could hear giggling.

But it wasn't *Mia's* giggle. It was . . .

Tuesday, December 29
5:30 P.M.
High Tea
Royal Genovian Gardens

Luisa!" I cried, throwing open the door.

Luisa was in my sister's bedroom, all right . . . with the duke!

The two of them were still in their bathing suits. Roger, the 12th Duke of Marborough, was snapping photos of Luisa with his cell phone as she jumped on Mia and Michael's bed, wearing the multimillion-dollar crown of Genovia. Beneath both their feet lay the Robe of State!

"Oh yeah," the duke was saying to Luisa. "You've got it. Work it, girl. Work it!"

Luisa saw me first, and stopped jumping with a startled jerk . . . so startled, in fact, that the crown snapped from her skull, and tumbled forward. Lucky for her—and the crown—Prince Khalil dashed up and caught it at the last minute, before it crashed to Mia's carpeted floor.

The duke, finally noticing us, lowered his cell phone and said, in his usual way-too-casual voice, "Oh hey, Leel, 'Livia. How's it going, dudes?"

I could hardly believe my eyes—let alone my ears. "How's it going? *How's it going?*"

"Now, Stick," Lady Luisa said, also sounding way too casual . . . but also a little scared. "Don't make too big a deal of this. We were only having some fun."

"On my sister's bed?" I nearly shouted. "In your bathing suits? *In her CROWN?!*"

"Oh my God," Luisa said, climbing down off the bed, accidentally kicking the Robe of State to an unceremonious heap on the floor. A sacred robe, woven and worn by my royal ancestors for centuries, was *lying on the floor*!!!

I'm not going to lie: I darted forward and picked it up. It was even heavier than I remembered, and now smelled of Luisa's suntan lotion.

"Trust you to make a way bigger deal out of this than it is," Lady Luisa said. "I mean, we were only—"

"It actually seems like kind of a big deal to me,"

Prince Khalil said. "To me—and I'm speaking as an out-sider, of course—it looks as if the two of you went into the Princess of Genovia's royal chambers without her per-mission, jumped on her bed, and photographed yourself wearing sacred royal symbols you had no right to touch."

"Sacred royal symbols?" the Duke of Marborough sneered. "Don't be a tool, okay? It's just a ratty old coat and a junky old crown."

"A junky old crown?" I almost exploded. "This *junky old crown*," I said, pointing at the crown Khalil held, "is worth over twenty million dollars and symbol-izes hundreds of years of historic leadership!"

"Whoa," the duke said. "Chill, Princess. You don't have to yell."

"I'll yell if I want to!" I yelled. I handed the robe to Prince Khalil. "Would you mind putting these away for me?" I asked. "They go over there." I pointed to the velvet box and dressmaker dummy in the corner.

"Sure," Prince Khalil said.

"Now," I said, turning back to Luisa and the duke. "Give me that phone."

"Don't do it, Roger!" Lady Luisa cried.

"Do it, Roger," I said. "Or I'll tell my sister everything, and she'll tell your parents."

The duke looked pale, and handed over Lady Luisa's phone.

"For heaven's sake," Luisa said, folding her arms across her chest. "Why do you always have to make such a big deal out of everything? No one in this family can take a joke."

"I can take a joke," I said, as I scrolled through her photos and deleted every one that featured Luisa in the royal crown of Genovia. "It just has to be funny."

"This joke was funny," Luisa said. "Or at least it was going to be, until you ruined it."

"Ha ha," I said, handing Luisa her phone back. All the photos were gone. "I can definitely see the humor in the situation."

"You can?" she asked hopefully.

"No," I said. "Luisa, you and the duke need to find your clothes and leave. Now."

Lady Luisa bristled. "You don't own this palace. You can't kick me out of it."

"Yes I can," I said. "When my dad and my sister aren't here, I'm in charge."

"Listen, Stick," Lady Luisa said, thrusting her pointy chin at me. "*We* were here way before you." By "we" I guess she meant her and the duke, and by "here" I guess she meant the palace, before I arrived from New Jersey.

"Well, I highly doubt my sister will ever invite you back if she hears about this . . ."

The duke looked scared. "But you said you wouldn't tell if I gave you the phone!"

"Don't listen to her, Roger. She wouldn't dare tell on us." Lady Luisa flipped her hair. "Only a stupid stick who can't take a joke would do something like that."

It's hard for me to write this even now, my fingers are shaking with so much rage. I was soooooo mad at her!

"You need to leave NOW!" I yelled, and finally Luisa looked scared. The duke looked terrified, too. Even Prince Khalil looked a little frightened. The only person, in fact, who didn't look scared was Serena, my bodyguard, who'd heard all the yelling and come upstairs to see what was going on, as is her professional duty.

I had Serena escort Lady Luisa and the duke out of the palace (and make sure they didn't touch any other artifacts of historical significance on their way out), and put them in separate royal cars back to their villas. I didn't want them enjoying a make-out session in the backseat on their way home.

"Are you going to tell your sister?" Prince Khalil asked me as we made our way back to the pool.

"Of course not," I said. "Mia's got enough to worry about without learning that someone broke into her bedroom and tried on the crown and the Robe of State, too."

Khalil looked thoughtful. "I don't know. I think maybe you should tell her. Maybe if you did, she'd know to keep her door locked from now on . . . especially when historical royal ceremonial objects are in her room."

It makes my heart hurt to think about us having to

keep our bedroom doors locked against intruders, like the palace is some kind of apartment building, or something.

"No," I said. "This was just a onetime thing. I'm sure it will never happen again."

"Well, hopefully not," he said. "But you never know."

But I did know. Luisa would never make the same mistake twice. She has a mean streak, but she isn't brainless. "It will be fine," I said.

I really thought that!

Then.

But when Prince Khalil and I got back to the pool, things got even worse. Everyone asked if we'd found Luisa and the duke, so I had to tell them a little white lie:

"We did," I said. "Luisa wasn't feeling well, so the duke took her home."

"Aw," Nishi said. "That's so romantic!"

"Well," I said. "If you call food poisoning romantic."

Prince Morgan looked panicky. "Oh no! What did she eat? Did I have any? I can't get ill. I've got the coronation on Thursday! I've got to look my best for the public."

Prince Morgan is convinced he's going to win the lawsuit, and that it's him who'll be crowned on Thursday. Right!

"No worries," I said. "She's on a juice cleanse."

I figured that was the most diplomatic way to put it. Prince Morgan looked very relieved.

I can't believe that out of everyone I babysat today, the person who always accuses ME of acting like a baby is the one who acted the most babyish and immature of all.

Even worse, it's Luisa I should have been keeping the closest eye on all day, not Purple Iris or the babies or even Prince Morgan. She's the one who needs the most looking after!

The only good thing to come out of this is that I think it's brought me and Prince Khalil closer. He's the only one who knows the truth.

And, despite my worries that I might have frightened him a bit with my yelling, he whispered a little while ago—while Grandmère was making me pour out the tea, which of course Purple Iris spilled all over the travertine tile—that he really admires the way I handled the situation.

"It reminded me of that ancestress of yours," he said.

"Really? Who?" I had no idea.

"Princess Rosagunde. The one who founded your royal family."

When I finally realized who he was talking about, I felt myself blush. I hope he's right. I'd love to have the blood of a warrior princess in my veins!

But all I feel like I have right now is a stomachache. I think I've eaten too many cucumber sandwiches.

Tuesday, December 29
6:30 P.M.
Royal Genovian Gardens

The news is not good. I knew it the minute Mia and Michael got home. I could tell by her face. My dad's wasn't much better.

Of course they're trying to act like everything is fine.

But if everything is fine, why is Prince Morgan's dad so happy? He and his wife, Princess Bella, are taking Morgan out to eat for dinner (I suppose it would be awkward for them to eat here with us when they're about to steal our home).

After Mia and Michael got done kissing the babies and saying how great they looked and what a good job we'd all done babysitting (and had sent Victorine and Marguerite and Prince Gunther and Princess Komiko and Nadia home, with thanks and generous tips for their services), Mia explained what had happened. The courts had heard all the evidence from both sides—ours and Cousin René's—and had been unable to come up with a ruling, so now the case is going to have to go before the Genovian Supreme Court, which will have an emergency session tomorrow.

"So we still don't know whether there'll be a coronation on Thursday?" I asked.

"No," Mia said. "Not for another twenty-four hours."

I thought I might break down and cry when I heard that, which really isn't like me. I'm not a highly emotional person. I am about *some* things, of course—catching my cousin in my sister's bedroom wearing the royal crown, for instance; or the fact that the glaciers are melting at such an accelerated rate that polar

bears are literally getting stranded on them with no food to eat, separated from their families, and starving to death.

Obviously *those* things make me want to cry.

But that we might have to wait another twenty-four hours before we know whether Mia is going to be crowned? That shouldn't make me feel weepy.

I'm probably just overtired from spending the whole day with little babies. I don't know how parents do it. Child-rearing is hard.

The worst part was saying good-bye to Prince Khalil.

He kissed me good night . . . on each cheek, like always, the standard Genovian hello and good-bye greeting. It takes a lot of getting used to for an American.

"Call me later and tell me what you decide to do about your cousin," he whispered.

"I will," I said, feeling lame. If I'd turned my head

just a tiny inch, I could have had my first kiss . . . on the lips!

But I was too much of a coward. What was it he'd been saying about me being like my ancestress, Princess Rosagunde? Ha! Wrong.

"And don't forget," he added with a smile, "I still have your gift! If I don't give it to you soon, it's going to be ruined."

What? What could my gift be that if he doesn't give it to me soon, it could be ruined? It certainly isn't a kiss, if that was the case. Kisses never go bad.

Oh well.

Dad has announced that he is barbecuing. Dad likes to barbecue when there's bad news, because he thinks it cheers people up.

Of course the exact opposite is true. Dad is a terrible cook (I'm not going to say this is because he's a prince who grew up in a palace never having to cook for himself, but the empirical data supports this).

It also drives Chef Bernard crazy when Dad decides to barbecue, because as a professional chef, it upsets him when anyone in the palace cooks except for him.

But Chef Bernard is pretending like he doesn't mind, and is cheerfully making all these side dishes to go with Dad's burgers, such as potato salad (only Chef Bernard can't make potato salad simply: he has to add beluga caviar to it. That is life in a palace).

Tuesday, December 29
7:00 P.M.
Royal Genovian Gardens

Uh-oh.

I'd decided NOT to tell my family about what Lady Luisa had done, because really, Luisa has enough problems: Her parents are still fighting over who *doesn't* get custody of her. She's in love with a boy who really isn't that good of a boyfriend to her. And she doesn't even have a sister or a stepbrother or a decent pet, like a dog or an iguana.

The last thing a girl like that needs is more trouble, even if she's practically a professional at making it for herself. I decided to give her a chance to apologize to me, or at least make it up to me by offering to not call me Stick anymore.

But it turned out I needn't have bothered. Because all of a sudden, as we were sitting there waiting for our cheeseburgers, Mia, who was scrolling through her phone, let out a gasp.

"Why, that little _____!"

I won't write the word that Mia said. All I'll say is that Grandmère was so startled, she choked on her side-car, the special cocktail that she likes to have before dinner. And it takes quite a lot to get Grandmère to choke on her sidecar.

"Language, Amelia, language," Grandmère said when she was done choking. "A royal always watches what she says, especially when there are little ones about."

Purple Iris, who was toddling close by, cried, "_____," in a loud, happy voice, a smile on her face.

"You see?" Grandmère said pointedly.

"Oh, Lana, I'm so sorry," Mia said to Purple Iris's mother, looking stricken. "It's just that I've received some dreadful news."

"Oh no!" Mrs. Rockefeller looked shocked. "You've heard from the Supreme Court already?"

"No, not that. One of our little cousins posted some photos on her social media that got picked up by Rate the Royals. They were photos of her in a bikini, wearing the royal crown while walking all over the Robe of State . . . in my bedroom!"

My heart nearly exploded out of my body, I was so shocked.

I wasn't the only one who was shocked, either. Michael went, "Do you mean *our* bedroom?"

"Yes, *our* bedroom," Mia said, and passed him her phone. "Look."

Michael looked at the photos. "Oh my."

"Now, now," Grandmère said, flicking through the photos on her own phone. "One almost has to admire the girl. She is quite photogenic. One should make the most of one's looks while one is young."

"Grandmère," Mia said. "That is hardly the point, and you know it. That's the royal crown she's wearing—with a bikini!"

"A fringed bikini," Michael's sister, Lilly, added. She was looking at Luisa's photos over his shoulder. "With sequins."

"I feel sorry for the girl," Helen Thermopolis said. "This is clearly a cry for attention."

"She has my attention," Rocky said.

"Ew!" Nishi yelled. "*Rocky!*"

"What?" he asked innocently.

I buried my face in my hands. I couldn't believe that, after how careful I'd been to delete the photos, I'd neglected to ask Luisa whether or not she'd already posted any to social media. Of *course* she had! She's Lady Luisa Ferrari! I should have asked her about that, and made her delete those, too. I was the worst babysitter— and member of the royal household—ever.

"What are we going to do?" Michael asked.

"Do?" Grandmère took a sip of her drink. "Nothing at all. Other than the fact that, if the subject comes up, we will remark how amusing it is that Lady Luisa came up with such a cunningly made counterfeit crown and robe for her little photo shoot."

"And what about the fact that she had her little photo shoot in *my* bedroom?" Mia demanded.

"*Our* bedroom," Michael said. "And no one's going to know that's our bedroom, Mia. It's not like we've ever allowed photographers in there."

"Of course they're going to know that's our bedroom," Mia said, enlarging one of the photos. "That's Fat Louie peeking out from under the bed there." Fat Louie is her cat. He is approximately twenty years old. He is quite popular with the Genovian press, due to his propensity to leap out from beneath the royal furniture and slash at the ankles of visiting dignitaries. For some reason, the media finds this delightful. "Poor thing. I wonder what he was thinking when those two kids were in there, jumping around. He must have been terrified."

"He'll have to get used to it," Michael said, lifting Baby Prince Frank from his bouncy seat, as he'd begun to fuss. "When these two start crawling, it will be even worse."

I couldn't believe I had forgotten to check on Fat

Louie's welfare while I'd been in Mia's room! I wasn't only a rotten babysitter, I was a rotten pet sitter, too.

And now everyone who saw those photos was going to know they were real. There's no mistaking Fat Louie. He is very distinctive.

Should I speak up and tell them that I'd caught Luisa and the duke in Mia and Michael's room? There didn't seem to be much point to it now, even though I could see Nishi eyeing me from across the table. She had to know that my little story about Luisa having to leave because of "food poisoning" had been made up.

But what good would my saying I'd been there do?

That's when Dad handed me a plate with a cheeseburger and potato salad with caviar on it. I could hardly eat it, I felt so sick, especially as I listened to the conversation around me.

"Obviously," Grandmère said, "the baroness will have to be informed."

The baroness! I forgot that she was in Biarritz! I'd kicked Lady Luisa out of the palace when she didn't even have a proper adult guardian to return home to!

"And the duke's parents, as well," Grandmère went on.

Mia sighed. "I agree. I think I should be the one to do it, to preserve your friendship with the baroness, Grandmère."

"Oh, no." Grandmère was already speed-dialing Luisa's grandmother, even though cell phone use at the table is an abomination. "I'm more than happy to inform the baroness that she needs to return home immediately and deal with her granddaughter's poor choices."

I felt something cold grip my heart.

"Wait a minute," I heard myself squeak. "You don't have to do that. I mean, yes, the baroness should probably come home immediately. But I think Luisa has been punished enough."

Everyone turned to look at me. The burger in my throat felt hard as a lump of clay, and not just because Dad, as usual, had burned it.

"Prince Khalil and I caught Luisa and Roger in your room," I said to Mia. "I didn't tell you because I thought I'd taken care of it. I deleted all the photos, and then Serena and I kicked them out of the palace. I honestly thought that would be the end of it. I didn't know Luisa had already posted some of the photos."

"It's true!" Nishi, who could tell how upset I was getting, nodded energetically. "She really did kick them out, Your Highnesses! Luisa *and* the duke. I mean, I didn't see it, but I saw Olivia afterward, and I could tell something bad had happened by how upset she looked. Only she said Luisa had food poisoning."

I loved Nishi right then. Even though she can be annoying sometimes, with her love for Dylan the cheater, her insistence on calling her period "shells," and her recent chumminess with Luisa, she really is a great best friend.

Grandmère nodded. "Very diplomatic of you, Olivia. It was kind of you not to embarrass your cousin any more than she'd already embarrassed herself by her own ill judgment."

Mia smiled. "Yes, I agree. Thank you, Nishi. And thank you, Olivia, for letting me know. I appreciate your honesty, and also your loyalty. It makes me feel much better to know that you were there, looking after our family's—as well as the throne's—best interests."

I felt myself blushing. If I'd been looking after the throne's best interests, none of it would have happened in the first place. Still, I murmured, "Of course," and tried not to feel too guilty.

"Nevertheless," Grandmère said in her most commanding voice, "that girl will have to be punished for committing such a violation against the sanctity of the throne. Might I suggest banishment?"

"No!" I cried. I don't really like Luisa, but I don't *hate* her.

"Now, Mother," Dad said as he scraped char off the grill. "Let's not go too far. She's only a child."

"Only a child? Are you trying to imply that children don't know what they're doing? Why, in your father's day, a child younger than Luisa shot at the invading Nazi forces with his rabbit-hunting gun from that window right there, and managed to hit an SS officer square in the shoulder, and later on, your father awarded that boy the Genovian Medal of Valor."

"Yay!" Rocky yelled. "Nazi stories!"

"Clarisse, please," Helen said. "No Nazi stories at the dinner table. Remember? You promised."

Grandmère scowled. "Fine. But you can't possibly allow the little minx to attend the coronation on Thursday. The press will have a field day."

"Well," Mia said, frowning. "Yes, that's certainly true."

The cold thing gripping my heart constricted. Luisa not attend the coronation? Luisa's only reason for living, practically, is occasions like the coronation, where she gets to dress up in her finest gowns by Claudio, her favorite designer, and show them off to her social media followers.

"I know what Luisa and the duke did was really, really bad," I said. "It was a huge violation of trust and also an insult during this very stressful time, what with Prince Morgan's dad suing us and all. He probably thinks we don't even know how to keep our crown jewels safe. But maybe we should think of some other kind of punishment for Luisa. Because not allowing her to come to the coronation really might—"

Kill her, was what I was going to say. And also make her hate me forever—more than she already does.

But it was too late, since both Mia and Grandmère

had already gotten on their phones and walked away from the table.

"Hello, Your Grace," Mia was saying into her phone. "It's Princess Amelia. So sorry if I interrupted your dinner, but I need to discuss something your son Roger did today while he was over at the palace. You might have seen some photos on Rate the Royals. It appears that Roger was the photographer . . ."

And Grandmère, over on her side of the room, was saying, "Baroness? Oh hello, it's me, Clarisse. How are you? Oh, the Hôtel du Palais? How simply divine. Well, I'm so sorry to have to rain on your *petite* parade, but I have something simply dreadful to tell you about your granddaughter . . ."

I sank back into my chair, feeling the cold thing slipping away and being replaced by something else.

"What's the matter?" Nishi asked, noticing my expression.

I sighed. "I've always tried to set an example by treating Luisa the way I'd want to be treated," I said. "And now look what's happened."

Nishi shoveled a large serving of caviar potato salad into her mouth. "Dude," she said, after she'd swallowed. "*You* didn't do anything wrong. *She* did."

"I know, but—"

"Whatever! Don't get me wrong, I like Luisa—some of the time, anyway—but that girl has no respect! She was in your *sister's room*! Your married sister's private room, that she shares with her husband! And a ten-thousand-year-old cat!"

"Twenty years old."

"Whatever. That cat could have been seriously injured. You don't go into married people's bedrooms, especially married princesses who rule—or are about to rule—your country. And you definitely don't put on their crown and jump on their bed and take photos. Plus, did you notice how she tried to abandon our babysitting business today to go play tennis with her boyfriend? What kind of a friend is that? So rude! Here." She handed me a macaron from the plate Chef Bernard had just brought out. "Eat one of these. You're right, they really are good."

I glanced at Nishi, smiling, and wondered how I could ever have feared—even slightly—last night that she liked Lady Luisa better than she liked me.

"Thanks, Nishi." I took the macaron and bit into it. It was lemon and vanilla, one of my favorites. "Thanks for everything."

"No problem," she said, and smiled back at me, her teeth full of macaron.

Wednesday, December 30
8:00 A.M.
Royal Genovian Bedroom

It's a gray, misty morning in Genovia (we do occasionally have those. We're a coastal community, after all), and I don't feel like getting out of bed. Partly it's because there's no reason to—without the sunshine there's no chance we'll be going to the beach or pool today; no riding Chrissy, my pony, either. She hates going out in the rain.

But also because my phone just chimed to let me know I've gotten a text.

<LadyLuisa

> I hate you.

That's all it said. Just *I hate you.*

But that's all she needed to say, really. I know what she means. Grandmère had told the baroness what Luisa had done—and that I'd witnessed it—and the baroness had not only immediately flown home from Biarritz, she'd told Luisa's parents.

If Princess Komiko is right, and Luisa's parents are arguing in their divorce settlement over who *doesn't* get custody of Luisa because neither of them want her, the news that Luisa had snuck into the Princess of Genovia's private bedroom and snapped photos of herself trying on the royal crown probably hadn't gone over too well. I bet her parents are now arguing over which military boarding school to send her to.

I thought about texting Luisa back *I hate you, too,* but that didn't seem like a very royal thing to do. Grandmère always says that a royal never expresses dislike for anything, even food one doesn't like. One merely spits it discreetly into one's napkin, then leaves the napkin at the side of one's plate.

Luisa is a food I don't particularly like, but I can't spit her out and leave her by the side of my plate because I'm related to her, and she also goes to the Royal Genovian Academy.

So unless her parents really do send her to military school, I'm going to have to see her again.

Which means I have to at least pretend to get along with her.

So instead of texting *I hate you, too,* I texted:

OlivGrace >

I'm sorry, Luisa. I really am.

This wasn't a lie. I *am* sorry. Sorry that she did something so foolish.

Then I wrote:

It probably would have been okay if you hadn't posted the photos online.

I waited to see if she'd write back. If she really, truly hated me, she wouldn't. Being hated by anyone, even someone like Luisa, is unpleasant. Grandmère is the only person I know who doesn't care about being disliked. And Grandmère says that's because enemies make things more interesting, and that she's been around so long that she has too many friends already. She doesn't have time for them all. She says she needs to start thinning out her social calendar, so she can have more time for naps.

< LadyLuisa

> You're still a stick, and you always will be.
>
> Prince Khalil thinks so, too. He told Roger.

WHAT? This caused me to sit straight up in my bed.

OlivGrace >

> What do you mean?

Roger's parents took away his gaming system as punishment and now Roger can't play Warhunt with Khalil and the rest of the boys. When Khalil asked why and Roger told him it's because you're a stick who squealed on us, Khalil said he was relieved he'd never kissed you. Now it will be easier for him to break up with you. Sorry not sorry. That's what he said.

I felt the cold thing from last night grip my heart again, only worse.

Of course I knew that Luisa was lying. Khalil would never call me a stick, especially to the Duke of Marborough.

Although Khalil and the duke *were* friends, and they *did* play video games together. *Warhunt* is one of Prince Khalil's favorites. I'd tried to play it with him one time, but it had seemed so pointless. In the game, one soldier has to stop the other soldier, who's gone rogue, from blowing up the rest of the soldiers. I thought this was a bit stupid. Why didn't the princess of the country just declare that the war was over and send all the soldiers home, and get mental health treatment for the rogue soldier?

Prince Khalil had said I was missing the point of the game, which I guess I was.

OlivGrace >

You're lying. Prince Khalil never said that.

< LadyLuisa

Yes he did. He said he was breaking up with you because you're a stick who's never been kissed or ever even had her "shells."

Now I knew she was lying. Why on earth would Prince Khalil break up with me because I hadn't had my period, let alone "shells," a word he couldn't even know meant period?

By this time I was so mad, I'd gotten out of bed and stormed across the room to open the curtains, accidentally tripping over Nishi on her air mattress because I'd forgotten she was still visiting.

"W-what's going on?" she asked sleepily, rubbing her eyes.

"Luisa says Prince Khalil is breaking up with me because I'm a stick who's never been kissed or had her period," I told her, pointing at my phone.

Nishi yawned. "Oh, her. Don't believe anything she says. She's just mad because she's in trouble for the thing with the crown."

"Right?" I sat back down on my bed. "Khalil was there. He saw what they did!"

"Exactly." Nishi brushed her long hair from her eyes. "What do you think Chef Bernard has made for breakfast? Chocolate croissants, I hope."

"I should just text Prince Khalil," I said, "and ask him, shouldn't I? I mean, if he really said that thing about breaking up with me. Not that we're going out. We're just friends, really."

"No!" Nishi was on her feet. She snatched my phone away from me. "Don't do that! Don't dignify

anything that cousin of yours says with a response. Why are you even talking to her? Torturing you is what she lives for."

"Yeah," I said. "I'm glad you're finally starting to notice. But I should text him anyway just to say good morning."

"Do you normally text him just to say good morning?"

"Well," I said. "No."

"Then why would you start now? Let him text you."

This made no sense to me. "Why?"

"Because it never hurts to let a boy wait." Nishi put my cell phone down her pants.

"Um, Nishi," I said. "I'm pretty sure that was a sexist statement. Also, what you just did is completely unhygienic. May I have my phone back?"

"Not right now. Too much screen time is bad for you. Let's go eat breakfast."

I decided not to argue with her. Nishi's been going out with Dylan longer than I've been going out with Prince Khalil, so she probably knows what she's doing.

Except the part where Dylan is a cheater and her parents hate him so much they took away her cell phone so she couldn't talk to him. Maybe Nishi *doesn't* know what she's doing.

Ugh.

Wednesday, December 30
Noon
Royal Media Room

We barely got two feet from my bedroom door before practically tripping over Prince Morgan. He was waiting in the hallway for us! Literally, he was sitting in the hall across from my bedroom door, playing video games on his phone.

"Excuse me, Your Highness and Miss Desai," Prince Morgan said very politely, climbing quickly to his feet. "I wanted to ask . . . uh . . . would you mind babysitting me again today?"

He wasn't alone, either. Guess who was with him?

"I bwush?" Purple Iris held up her tiny baby brush. "I pay wif big kids? I bwush?"

"NO!" I practically yelled, and tried to escape as quickly as possible by climbing onto the banister of the Grand Staircase (to slide down it, a technique Rocky and I have perfected over the months that we've lived here).

Unfortunately, Nishi stopped me.

"Hang on, Olivia," she whispered. "What would your grandmother say if we ignored this amazing business opportunity?"

"That we were doing the right thing," I said. "It's as important to protect your mental health as it is your physical health." This is the excuse Grandmère often gives for why she has to leave the palace whenever Helen Thermopolis's parents come to visit from Indiana.

"No," Nishi said. "I think we need to pursue this journey to its exciting and final conclusion."

"Where did you get that line?" I asked her. "*The Bachelor*?"

"No," she said. "Well, maybe."

"You only want to do it for the money," I said, careful to whisper so that the prince wouldn't overhear me. I didn't want to hurt his feelings.

"Well, of course, Olivia," Nishi whispered back. "But also because it's the right thing to do. And isn't that what you're always saying you want to do—the right thing?"

It was true . . . I *did* always want to do the right thing. And it was also true that before he'd met us, Prince Morgan had rarely—if ever—interacted with kids his own age, only his phone and his parents and his tutors . . . not to mention whoever made his butterscotch sundaes. We'd introduced a whole new world to him! That had to have been a good thing.

I glanced at the kid, who was shifting his weight from one foot to the other, staring at us eagerly.

"I bwush," Purple Iris said hopefully, holding up her brush. "I pay wif big kids?"

"Okay," I said to Prince Morgan and Purple Iris. "We'll babysit you again today. Come on. We're going down to the kitchens to see what's for breakfast."

Prince Morgan's face lit up.

"Do you think Prince Gunther could come over again, too?" he asked. "I know we can't play water polo, since it's raining. But perhaps we could do something else? Anything else."

"Uh," I said, exchanging an amused glance with Nishi. "Sure. We could invite Prince Gunther over again."

Prince Gunther would love it.

"And maybe we could invite Prince Khalil, as well," I said. "You liked him, didn't you, Prince Mor—OW!"

The "ow" was because Nishi had stepped on my foot, and given me a warning glance. "Prince Khalil can come over anytime he wants," she said. "But he has to text first. That's how these things work."

Wow. I didn't know all these rules about dating. I thought anyone could text first. It's no wonder Prince Khalil and I have never kissed.

Now we're all in the royal media room (well, all of us minus the babies and Prince Khalil—the babies because the nanny is back from her vacation today, and Prince Khalil because he still hasn't texted), where we're watching the unauthorized biopics of my sister, Mia's, life (Nishi got them for me for Christmas, and is the one who insisted on watching them).

The adults aren't here, of course. For one thing, Mia doesn't like the unauthorized movies based on her life (she says they are highly inaccurate), and for another, they're all too busy strategizing about what to do if the decision from the Supreme Court goes the wrong way.

I think Purple Iris is a little bored, but there are enough scenes in the movies with cats and dogs that she's mostly behaving pretty well. I can sort of see what Mia means about the inaccuracies, because for some reason the filmmakers decided to include a lot of stuff about Fat Louie and Grandmère's dog, Rommel.

Only they didn't cast animals that actually look like

Fat Louie or Rommel. Possibly they couldn't find a twenty-pound orange tabby cat that likes to eat socks, or a hairless miniature poodle.

Midway through the last film, Grandmère came into the media room, curious about what we were doing.

Then she saw what we were watching.

"Oh," she said. "*My.*"

Grandmère has never been the biggest fan of the unauthorized biopics of Mia's life, but since she likes the actress they cast to play her, she stuck around, commenting on the many inaccuracies in the writing, mainly her love life and Genovia's location, which is erroneously stated as being situated between France and Spain. As every educated schoolchild knows, Genovia is between France and Italy.

I kind of thought that I would have heard from Prince Khalil by now.

I guess it's not so weird that I haven't, though. It's not like we've ever texted each other every minute of the day. We live our own independent lives. We each have our own interests, after all. We're not some crazy, mushy, married couple like Mia and Michael, who I sometimes see making out by the fountain at night, even though they have their own bedroom.

The fact that Prince Khalil hasn't called doesn't in any way make what Luisa said true.

Right?

Right???

Wednesday, December 30
6:00 P.M.
Royal Dining Room

It's six o'clock, and we still haven't heard anything from the Genovian Supreme Court.

I haven't heard anything from Prince Khalil, either . . . at least according to Nishi, who is still holding my phone (though in her pocket, not her panties) to make sure I don't call him.

"It's important not to appear needy," she says.

"I don't think Princess Olivia could ever appear needy," Prince Morgan says, coming to my defense. I'm really beginning to like this kid. He's been growing on me more and more, especially since he let Purple Iris brush his hair and "braid" it (which to her means put it in a butterfly clip). Prince Gunther let her do the same thing. They both look absolutely adorable.

"I don't know, Nishi," I say. "I'm starting to think this whole not-letting-me-call-him thing is stupid, because playing games in relationships is childish. It's like something my cousin Luisa would do."

"What would your cousin Luisa do?" Prince Gunther bounds up and asks. He has Purple Iris on his shoulders. She's riding him like a pony. In fact, her nickname for him is "Pince Pony" (since she can't say the word "prince").

"Nothing," Nishi says quickly. "Just girl talk."

Prince Gunther frowns. "I hate that. Why does there have to be girl talk and boy talk? Why can't all talk be for everyone?"

I realize he has a point.

"Yeah," I say. "What about that? Why can't all talk be for everyone?"

"If all boys were as nice as Prince Gunther, that would be fine," Nishi says. "But they aren't."

Prince Gunther is so startled by this unexpected compliment that he stumbles, a bit like a pony that's seen a snake (ponies are deathly afraid of snakes).

Fortunately, Purple Iris, who is clinging to his hair, manages to hang on safely without falling off. "Whoa!" she cries. "Bad pony. Bad pony!"

"You think I am nice?" Prince Gunther asks Nishi in an astonished voice once he's recovered himself.

"Well," she says, blushing a little. "I mean . . . yes. Of course. A little."

"Only a little?" Prince Gunther asks teasingly.

"Well," Nishi says, lowering her eyelashes like one of her beloved Disney princesses. "Maybe more than a little . . ."

I can't believe this. Nishi is flirting with Prince Gunther . . . but she has a boyfriend back in New Jersey for whom she got her cell phone taken away! Nishi's boyfriend, Dylan, is the whole reason we're babysitting these little royals in the first place.

Meanwhile, she still won't give me back my phone.

I was never sure her relationship with Dylan made her such an expert in the social sciences anyway, especially since he's a cheater (on tests, anyway).

But who even cares? Whether or not my friend-who-is-a-boy still likes me is hardly as important as who will one day rule the country in which I live.

Guests have been arriving all day for tomorrow's coronation, and may I say that it is a bit awkward that we still don't know whether there'll even be a ceremony for them to attend?

But of course Mia keeps saying, "Everything is going to be fine, just fine!" and smiling and laughing.

I know this is all a big act, however. Not only because as soon as the guests turn their backs as they're led away to their rooms by the majordomo, Mia completely stops smiling, but also because Lilly told me a secret: when Mia is lying, her nostrils flare.

I looked super close at Mia's face, and it's true: every time Mia says everything is going to be fine, her nostrils flare all over the place!

My sister definitely doesn't think everything is going to be fine . . . and I'm starting to agree. I could tell when Cousin René came to pick up Prince Morgan to take him out for dinner—we all agreed it probably wouldn't be best for the Albertos to dine with us tonight. He had the biggest grin on his face. Things obviously went much better in court for Prince Morgan's family than it did for mine!

"Over my dead body will Prince Morgan be crowned ruler of Genovia!" Dad keeps saying.

"Dad, honestly, I hung out with him all day today," I say. "He's a little spoiled, but not so bad."

"Not so bad?" Dad looks like he can hardly believe it. "Not so bad? Do you have any idea how much I've paid for all this, Olivia?"

By "all this" he means everything tomorrow—including all the fireworks and the food at the post-coronation ball. It's all being paid for out of our personal estate.

"No Alberto is going to enjoy chrysanthemums or beef Wellington purchased with *our* money," Dad says.

Chrysanthemums are those type of fireworks that explode into great big, round balls of sparkly light.

They look just like the flowers they're named after. They're basically the best fireworks, and they cost a *lot*.

"Dad, remember your blood pressure," Mia says.

"And also what the royal physician said about eating too much salt," says Helen.

But it's too late. Dad has already eaten around four bags of salt-and-vinegar chips (his favorite).

I totally understand. Even though I don't dislike Prince Morgan as much as I used to, I've eaten twenty-four Genovian macarons in assorted flavors. It's *hard* not to eat when you're—

Wednesday, December 30
10:00 P.M.
Royal Bedroom

I had to stop writing before because a royal courier walked in with a letter.

EVERYTHING IS DIFFERENT NOW!!!!!

Not just because of the letter. I got a phone call, too!!!!!!

But first, the letter:

It had the wax seal of the Genovian Supreme Court on it. So I knew it could only be one thing . . . the ruling about whether Mia would be crowned tomorrow!

I don't know about anyone else, but I was practically

holding my breath as I watched her break open the seal, then read what was written inside.

"Well?" Dad asked anxiously. "What does it say?"

A huge smile spread across Mia's face. This time, her nostrils didn't flare. "It says that the Renaldo family is the one and only true heir to the throne of Genovia."

Everyone in the room cheered—which of course woke the sleeping twins, who started to cry. But no one cared. Mia hugged Michael, who lifted her up and spun her around. Dad, seeing this, tried to do the same thing to Helen, but she cried for him not to, saying, "Your back! You'll throw it out again, Phillipe."

But Dad didn't care about his back any more than he cared about the crying babies. He swung Helen around anyway.

Rocky whooped, gave me a high five, then a down low, and then a fist bump. Then he grabbed hands with me and Nishi and made a ring around Grandmère, pulling us around her, chanting, "We're number one, we're number one," the way he does whenever his soccer team wins a game at school.

I will admit, this was kind of fun.

"Children, please," Grandmère said. But I could tell from her smile that she was delighted. "You're making me nauseous. And such flagrant displays of celebration are vulgar. Kindly remember that a good sport accepts both his wins and losses with grace."

"But Grandmère," Rocky yelled, "we don't have to move out of the palace!" which caused Grandmère's smile to turn into a frown.

"And what," she said, "would have been so wrong with that? A great many people don't live in palaces and are perfectly content. I believe you yourself spent

most of your life living in a downtown New York City loft apartment. Were you unhappy then?"

"No," Rocky admitted, pretending that a bust of an ancient relative of ours was a basketball hoop and going for an imaginary jump shot. "But I didn't have my own pool or billiards room."

"The mark of a truly royal person is one who can live happily without material things and still do good works for those less fortunate," said Grandmère.

Although I noticed Grandmère looked pretty relieved, probably because she doesn't have to give up her chaise longue next to the pool, upon which she can be found most mornings, soaking up the Genovian sun.

"I don't understand," Nishi said. "How could Prince Morgan's family have lost the lawsuit? I thought his DNA was a ninety-nine-point-nine genetic match to Princess Rosagunde's."

"It is, but that wasn't the only parameter the court took into account while making their ruling," Lilly said. She was looking over the letter that the court had sent over. "Royal succession has never been as simple or straightforward as inheritance based on blood."

"Absolutely," Grandmère said with a nod. "How could the courts overlook the fact that Renaldos have been toiling for centuries to insure that Genovia is one of the best places on earth to live? That its roads and hospitals and schools are the finest, that its people are well fed and cared for, and that its hotels and restaurants are rated the highest in the world on TripAdvisor?"

"Well, that," Lilly said, "and the fact that Prince Morgan's parents violated the law by breaking into the crypt of Princess Rosagunde and removing her DNA without state permission."

My jaw dropped when I heard this. "They *did*?"

"Shocking but true," Mia said, as she fussed over the babies to get them back to sleep. "I'm quite certain Cousin René defiling one of our most sacred and historic landmarks didn't help his claim with the court that he would be the best ruler of Genovia."

I shook my head. I was glad we had won the lawsuit, but all I could think about was poor Prince Morgan.

"Will Cousin René go to jail?" I asked.

"Unlikely," Lilly said. As a lawyer, she would know. "But he'll probably have to pay a fine for desecrating a national monument—and a princess's final resting place."

Before I had a chance to think about how truly awful it was that Prince Morgan's dad had *broken into a grave* to steal a princess's DNA in an attempt to make his son the ruler of Genovia, Nishi raced up to me and held out my phone.

"It's *him*," she said breathlessly.

It may sound stupid, but my heart skipped a beat when she held up my phone and the screen was flashing PRINCE KHALIL. *Accept? Decline?*

He'd called. HE'D FINALLY CALLED.

Of course I hit accept and then ran out the French doors into the garden so I could have some privacy, and also so that I could hear him, because the babies were crying again.

"Hello?"

"Olivia?" His voice sounded amazing, as nice and friendly as always, and not at all like he hated me. "Hi, it's me. I just heard about the ruling. Congratulations!"

"Oh, thanks," I said, trying to sound cool. Why was I trying to sound cool? I don't know. All of a sudden I felt kind of nervous talking to him, which isn't like me, because why should I be nervous talking to my friend-who-is-a-boy? "Yeah, we're really happy about it."

"You should be," he said. "How crazy was that cousin of yours for digging up your ancestor's grave?"

"Ha," I said. I had to stand under an ornately carved gargoyle of a prancing lion coming out of the palace wall to keep from getting wet. It had been raining all day, and there was a jet of water shooting out of the lion's mouth, but none of it was hitting me. "I know, right? Pretty gross."

"So I guess there's going to be a coronation ceremony tomorrow after all," he said.

"I guess so," I said.

"So I'll see you there?"

"Yes," I said. "I mean, I have to be there. I'm carrying the train of the Robe of State for my sister."

"Right," he said. Now his voice didn't sound so friendly anymore. "Olivia, are you mad at me, or something?"

"Me?" I was surprised. "No. Why would I be mad at you? I thought *you* were mad at *me*."

"Why would I be mad at you?" he asked. "You're the one who had a bunch of people over today and didn't invite me."

A bad feeling crept over me. It felt as if the stream of rain from the lion gargoyle's mouth was shooting down my back, even though I was standing well away from it. My shoulders hunched up as I pressed my phone to my ear.

"How did you know about that?" I asked.

"Because Gunther posted all these photos on his social media," Prince Khalil said, "of him hanging out at the palace today with you and Nishi and that Prince Morgan kid. You guys were watching movies or something. It looked like you were having fun."

My shoulders hunched even more. I felt terrible. At school they were always warning us not to post photos of ourselves on social media having fun with one another, because someone somewhere who hadn't been invited was going to see the photo and feel sad or left out.

Only that lesson had never sunk in for Prince Gunther. It wasn't his fault, necessarily. He just got carried away sometimes, like Purple Iris with the brushing.

"I didn't ask you because Luisa told me you wanted to break up," I said, feeling lame as the words were coming out of my mouth. I realized now that following Nishi's relationship advice had been a terrible idea. Prince Gunther was right: there shouldn't be girl talk or boy talk. It was important to be honest.

"Break up with you?" Prince Khalil's voice cracked. "Why would I break up with you?"

"Because you were mad about how I squealed on Luisa and the duke for being in my sister's bedroom," I said, blushing. I couldn't believe I'd said "break up with me." Prince Khalil and I weren't exactly going out, because we'd never even been on a date. So how could we break up?

Why oh why had I believed for one second anything Luisa had said, let alone allowed Nishi to keep me from calling Prince Khalil all day?

"I wasn't mad about that at all," Prince Khalil said.

"I thought you did the right thing. How could you have thought something so awful about me? And why would you listen to anything your cousin said, anyway?"

"I don't know." I wanted to go stand under the jet of water coming from the gargoyle's mouth and let its cool stillness put out the fire in my cheeks. But my cell phone wasn't waterproof. "It's just that Luisa said you and the duke were playing *Warhunt*, and that you—"

"*Warhunt*? I haven't seen Roger since I was at your house! I've been home all day, helping my auntie set up her new computer."

Now I felt even worse. "Oh. Well, I didn't know that."

"Well, you would have," Prince Khalil said, "if you'd called."

That pricked at my pride. "Well," I said. "You could have called me, too."

"How could I? I thought you were mad at me, since you were having a party and didn't invite me."

What was happening? Were we having our first fight?

"It wasn't a party," I assured him, grasping at anything to keep what I was pretty sure was happening from happening. "It was just more babysitting. Prince Morgan asked for Prince Gunther to be there."

"And not me?"

Oh no. Now I'd hurt his feelings!

"He asked for you, too," I lied smoothly. Grandmère says it's okay to lie if it makes someone feel better. "But I really did think you were mad at me, so I said you were busy."

"Well," Prince Khalil said, sounding only slightly less wounded. "I guess Luisa got what she wanted."

I was confused. "And what was that?"

"Drama. It's her favorite thing."

I couldn't help feeling even more terrible. It was true. Once again, my awful cousin had won.

"But at least we realized what she was up to before any permanent damage occurred," I said, more hopefully than I felt. "Right?"

"Sure," he said, but he didn't sound as convinced as I'd have liked. "Look, I have to go. My mom is calling me."

He wasn't lying, either. I did hear a woman's voice in the background calling his name. Maybe. It was hard to be sure with all the rain.

"Okay," I said. "But I'll see you tomorrow, right? At the coronation?"

"Yes," he said. "Bye."

And then he hung up. He actually hung up!

This was a wholly unsatisfactory conversation, and not just because I had it standing in the rain (well, practically standing in the rain). I think Prince Khalil and I just had our first fight.

Only it wasn't a fight, really. Because we both agreed I'd made a terrible decision, believing anything Luisa said.

It left a terrible weight between my already hunched-up shoulders. Nishi noticed as soon as I walked back into the dining room.

"What's the matter?" she asked, her smile fading. She thought I'd come in bubbling over with happiness, like any girl whose crush had finally called. "Is everything okay?"

"Sure," I said. I didn't want to tell Nishi what was wrong, especially since I didn't even know what was wrong. Maybe nothing. "Everything's fine."

Except that unlike my sister, Mia, my nostrils

didn't flare when I said it. Everyone thinks I really am okay.

And I am. Mostly.

I'm just not looking forward to tomorrow as much as I was before.

And it's all Luisa's fault.

And maybe a little bit mine, as well.

Thursday, December 31
10:30 A.M.
Royal Bedroom

I can't believe I'm writing this. Or that I'm about to write what I'm going to write . . .

I mean, I knew the moment I woke up that it wasn't going to be a good day. It was still raining, for one thing, and you know what they say (or at least what Grand-mère says): "Rain on coronation day means marauders can't be far away."

Except that I highly doubt marauders are on their way to steal the throne from Mia. Cousin René already tried that, and all he got for his pains was a one-way ticket back home to Italy (although Prince Morgan left me the sweetest thank-you note, saying how much he hoped we could hang out again sometime. I guess he doesn't realize what the word "babysit" means—that his parents were paying us to hang out with him the whole time. Cousin René sure doesn't: he left without paying his share of our babysitting money).

Anyway, what happened after I woke up was even worse—in some ways—than marauders invading the palace, or people not paying you the money they owe you.

Which is that this morning when Francesca, my wardrobe consultant, came in with my gown to start getting ready for the coronation and I went into the bathroom to bathe, I discovered I'd finally gotten my period.

At first I thought I'd fallen asleep eating raspberry macarons in bed again (yes . . . this has actually happened before).

But then I remembered that Nishi and I had finished all the macarons downstairs, before we'd gone to bed.

For a minute I swear I thought I was dying, even though I'm already very well-read on the biological mechanics of the female mammalian reproductive system.

It's just a bit of a shock when it happens to *you* . . . especially when you've been waiting so long.

And it's happened to everyone around you.

And your own cousin keeps harping at you about it.

And your best friend keeps calling it "shells."

And then when it finally happens to you, it happens ON YOUR SISTER'S CORONATION DAY.

You hardly expect it *then*.

But of course that's always when things happen: when you least expect—or want—them.

Obviously I was completely unprepared and had no idea what to do (even though everyone in the entire household—except my dad—has discussed it with me multiple times, especially Mia, because they are so anxious to make sure I don't freak out when it does happen).

But there I was, freaking out (well, only a little). This was the big moment, and I couldn't remember what I was supposed to do.

Of course all I had to do was poke my head out of

the bathroom and ask Nishi or even Francesca if I could borrow a tampon.

But for some reason I didn't want them to know. Not yet. I knew they'd make a huge fuss and congratulate me and probably kiss me and in Nishi's case demand a selfie, and I just couldn't handle it.

So instead I stuffed a wad of toilet paper in my pants and told Francesca I'd be right back, that I needed to see Grandmère about something, then went down the hall to see her.

I found her in her room sitting at her vanity table, putting on her lipstick and eyebrows for the day. Because the coronation was such a huge event, she was making her face look extra fancy.

"Hi, Grandmère," I said, sitting on a poofy chair beside her.

"Well, good morning, darling," she said, lowering her eyebrow pencil so she could get a good look at my reflection in her enormous vanity mirror. "Why are you still dressed in your pajamas? Are you ill? You look a bit peaked."

"No," I said. "I'm not ill. It's just that . . . well . . ."

"If it's something concerning that boy," Grand-mère said, "I wouldn't worry. He's quite smitten with you."

I was really surprised that she knew anything was amiss between Khalil and me. I'd been careful to pretend everything was fine, just fine.

"Okay," I said, not believing for a second that she was right. "Thanks, Grandmère. But I just thought I should tell someone, and I'm sure Mia and Helen are pretty busy . . . I had my period this morning."

Grandmère had gone back to drawing on her eyebrows, and when I said the thing about my period, she  accidentally jerked her hand so the black line went running all the way up the middle of her forehead. This startled Rommel, who'd been watching both of us from Grandmère's bed, and he let out a little yelp.

"Darling!" Grandmère cried, reaching for a tissue to wipe off the line. "That's wonderful! Is it your first time?"

"Yes," I said.

I wasn't surprised Grandmère had forgotten. She forgets a lot of stuff, like how old she is, what year it is, where she put her scepter, and who is the president of the United States (which to her doesn't matter, since she doesn't live there).

I know menstruation is a natural process, but I still wasn't all that comfortable discussing it with my grandmother, even though of course I really love her.

"Of course, I could talk to Mia or Nishi or Helen about it," I said, "but they'll make too big a fuss. And I really don't want to mess up my white gown for the coronation today—"

"Oh darling, don't worry," Grandmère said, waving a hand. "They have pills for it now, you know, to make it go away."

"*Really?*" How, with my extensive reading on the subject, had I missed this?

"Yes, of course, darling. You don't think lady astronauts and professional tennis players and these actresses who do all those stunts in bikinis mess about with their periods, do you?"

"Uh . . . I don't know."

"Well, they don't. You might have to wait until you're a bit older, though, before they'll give them to you. But I'm sure if you discuss it with Helen Thermopolis"—Grandmère always says my stepmom's name as if it tastes a bit like spinach—"she'll be more than happy to talk about your options."

This was heartening news. I wondered why Luisa didn't know about the pills. She always knew everything that was on the cutting edge. Or maybe she did know, and preferred all the attention she got from asking to borrow tampons every two to three days.

"In the meantime, go over to my bathroom," Grandmère said, gesturing toward her enormous en suite, which featured a tub so large five people could fit in it. "I'm sure you'll find what you're looking for in there. It's been ages for me, but I know Maxine"—her maid—"keeps it fully stocked for her own little emergencies. You know what to do, don't you? Or do you need a demonstration?"

I shook my head. In school they'd separated the girls from the boys, then shown us a film. It had been hilariously bad. Nadia had said afterward that in her former country, where she'd worked as a child actress, she'd starred as the girl character in the educational film they'd shown her class.

"When my character got her period," Nadia told us, laughing at the memory, "the director had me stand at the side of the lake and look sad while all my character's friends splashed around in the water and had fun. It was so dumb!"

I'd laughed along with everyone else at the story, but now that it's happened to me, I sort of know how Nadia's character felt. I understand how to use the pads, but tampons are a little too much for me right now. Maybe tomorrow.

"How are you feeling?" Grandmère asked as I came out of her bathroom.

"Okay, I guess." I sat back down on her poofy chair. "It's complicated."

"Oh yes." Grandmère had successfully drawn on both eyebrows and also put on lipstick and looked less scary than before. "Womanhood is complicated indeed."

"No, that's not what I mean," I said. "I mean I

thought I'd feel different after getting my—you know. Because of being a woman now, and all. But I don't."

Grandmère nodded and reached for her lipstick. "No. Because that's not what makes someone into a woman."

"It isn't?" I watched as she applied the bright red rouge to her cheeks. "Then what does?"

"Life, my dear," she said, and regarded her reflection. "Life. Now, you'd better hurry along to your room and get ready. You'll want to eat a good breakfast this morning. You will need all your strength to carry the ends of that wretched robe down the aisle this afternoon. I didn't want to say anything in front of Rocky, but the truth is, despite the cleaning, it really does smell a bit like farts."

"Yes," I said. "You're right."

So I did exactly as she suggested. After all, she's had a lot more experience at this royal thing than anyone else I know.

Thursday, December 31
12:45 P.M.
Grand Staircase

Well, it's about to happen—the day I was beginning to think would never come.

We're all here (by "we" I mean me, Mia, the prime minister, my dad, all the television cameras—from thirty-nine different countries—and all the guests, but they're still being seated inside the throne room).

Of course Michael and Dad and Helen and Rocky and Grandmère are here, too, since they're taking part in the procession. Nishi was disappointed that she's not participating in the ceremony (she had been a junior bridesmaid in Mia's wedding), and so had to sit in the audience with Prince Gunther and everyone else, but I'm a little relieved, actually: she found out about my "shells" when I had to change my pad and has talked of (almost) NOTHING ELSE since.

"Oh my God, Olivia!" she kept whispering all through breakfast. "Maybe we'll both get it at the same time!"

"Please," I whispered back. "Stop talking about it."

"And your sister paid me," she hissed. "She just slipped me the cash this morning. Ten euros per hour per kid . . . including Prince Morgan, since his dad skipped out on the bill! She said she felt bad about it."

"I know," I said. She'd paid me, too.

"I can get my cell phone!" Nishi said. "And call Prince Gunther whenever I want!"

This confused me. "Prince Gunther? What about Dyl—?"

"I'm seeing Prince Gunther later, at the after-party! And you'll be seeing Prince Khalil later, too!"

"Yes I will. But—"

"It's so exciting!"

Nishi can hardly contain herself. I keep telling her it's a post-coronation luncheon, not an after-party, but she doesn't care.

"Maybe he'll give you his gift then," Nishi keeps going on. "Maybe his gift really is a kiss!"

I already know Khalil's gift isn't a kiss, since he said it was something that could be "ruined" if he didn't give it to me sooner rather than later.

And I also know from our last conversation that the chance of us kissing is about zero, since we're barely even friends anymore, thanks to Luisa and her evil games.

But I don't want to mention this to Nishi, since she's having such a good time.

"Oh my God," Nishi breathed excitedly over her Belgian waffles. "What if you get your first kiss and your first shells on the same day? And then Prince Gunther kisses *me*? That would be so romantic!"

I love Nishi, but it was all I could do to keep from flinging myself away from the table, going back to bed, and pulling the covers up over my head.

But it's okay, because she's gone now. She has my

cell phone, with which she's sworn she'll record the ceremony for me, so I can watch how it looks from the audience (even though of course it's going to be on every major news network later).

Mia looks really beautiful. The dress Sebastiano designed for her is perfect. He wanted to try to hide the baby weight that she hasn't lost, but Mia said, "Why should I hide it? I'm proud of it. I have two healthy babies, and I'm about to be crowned ruler of my country. I'm a strong, powerful woman. Make me a gown that emphasizes that."

So he did. When she came gliding down the stairs just now, she looked like a ship about to set sail and conquer a million armies. Emblazoned with tiny white crystals that sparkled in the sunlight (the rain has finally stopped), she looked more like an empress than a princess.

"Wow." Michael was waiting with the rest of us at the bottom of the stairs. "Would you marry me?"

"Too late," Mia said, giving him a peck on the cheek. "I'm taken. So who's going to help me get this

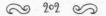

thing on?" She meant the Robe of State, which was being carried behind her by two very strong Genovian footmen. They were sagging under its weight a little. I'm telling you, that thing is really heavy (and smelly).

"I'll help," I said, as Rocky leapt forward to help as well. Rocky loves state events because it gives him a chance to wear his military attire. He is a junior officer in the Royal Genovian Guard, and during state events, he gets to wear a miniature sword at his side, which he always swears solemnly he will never draw and stab anyone with. So far, he never has.

But the Robe of State was too heavy for Rocky and me alone to lift to Mia's shoulders. Michael, Dad, and the footmen had to help.

"That thing is going to give you both backaches," Helen said worriedly, looking from me to Mia as we tried to straighten out the yards of red velvet and ermine. "Why does it have to be so heavy?"

"It represents the weight of the people," Mia said, "and my responsibility to them. I'll be fine, Mom. What about you, Olivia?"

I could tell by the look of concern she gave me that she'd heard about my "morning visitor." I knew Grandmère wouldn't have told her. She's good at keeping my secrets.

But probably Maxine, Grandmère's maid, had blabbed. It's impossible to keep anything secret in a palace.

"I'm fine," I said firmly. I feel fine, too, except for some slight discomfort in the midriff area. But that could be due to the fact that I ate four waffles for breakfast, so now my gown is a little tight in the waist.

"Excellent," Mia said, and pushed a bit at the bun into which her stylist, Paolo, had swept her hair. You could tell that it felt as restrictive as my waistline. But she had to wear her hair like that, so the royal crown would stay on when Dad laid it upon her head. "Shall we?"

Inside the throne room, the orchestra is playing the Genovian national anthem. Outside, I can hear all the people beyond the palace gates screaming Mia's name. It really is a happy occasion.

Too bad my heart is drumming so hard I can hardly

write this. I don't care anymore about the news cameras. I'm so used to them, they don't bother me.

But somewhere out in that throne room is Prince Khalil.

I just really hope it's true that he doesn't hate me.

Well, here goes.

Friday, January 1
Midnight
Royal Bedroom

HE DOESN'T HATE ME.

I don't know why I ever thought he did. I guess when someone like Lady Luisa Ferrari messes with your brain, you start thinking all sorts of crazy things.

Or maybe it was all the stress this past week, or of just generally being a royal. I thought carrying a bridal train was hard at Mia's wedding? Carrying a Robe of State is *ridiculous*.

Plus I had my own gown to worry about. I was convinced my pad was going to leak and I was going to have embarrassing stains all over the back of it. These are things girls actually have to worry about when they become women (not that I'm a woman yet . . . but, well, I'm closer than I've ever been).

But it turns out I needn't have worried. Everything turned out fine—at least as far as the ceremony went. Mia said her solemn vows to the prime minister and archbishop, promising to:

- Serve the Genovian people until death.
- Rule with wisdom and with grace.
- Be just and fair.
- Protect the monarchy and all within it.
- Devote her whole self to the country and the crown (although knowing Mia, she'll give at least some of herself to the twins and Michael and the rest of us, too).
- Severely punish those who throw fish heads into Genovian waters and pollute them.

(This last one is mentioned at every Genovian state event, because fish heads polluting the waters of

Genovia used to be a very big problem. It's not the case anymore now that Genovian oranges and olive oil are the number one exports, but it's tradition to mention the fish heads.)

It was after the last part that Mia knelt in front of Dad, and he transferred the crown—the one Luisa had taken photos of herself in—from his head to Mia's. There were tears in his eyes as he did this. Not because he was sad to be giving up the throne, he told us later, but because his little girls were growing up so fast.

Then the prime minister declared Mia the new princess regent of Genovia . . . and everyone cried, "Long live the princess!"

I really thought the palace rafters were going to fall down, everyone was cheering so loudly. I guess it's nice to have something to celebrate after a week of so much uncertainty. Things in the world haven't been that great either, so when something nice happens, people have a tendency to really, really want to applaud it.

I even saw Cousin René and his wife and Prince Morgan in the crowd applauding along with everyone else (although Cousin René wasn't doing so quite as enthusiastically). I thought they'd gone back to Italy, but Prince Morgan caught me today at the luncheon and said, "I told my dad I didn't want to go, because I like you so much! I said that if he made me go, I'd just get in my electric car and drive straight back here. So he said we could stay."

Aw! So sweet!

"'Tay," repeated Purple Iris, who was following Prince Morgan around, her favorite hairstyling item clutched in her hand. "I bwush? I pay wif big kids?"

"Oh, gee," I said. "That's so great. Why don't you go play with Nishi and Prince Gunther?" I pointed to my best friend and the prince, who were over by the fountain with all my other friends, laughing and having a good time together. I got the feeling from the way Nishi kept putting her hand on Prince Gunther's biceps that old cheating Dylan was permanently out of the picture. "I have someone I need to speak to . . ."

Because I'd seen someone else in the throne room who I'd wanted to have a word with . . . someone who'd smiled at me from the audience as I'd walked by, holding the ends of the Robe of State. Someone who started walking toward me later, at the luncheon in the royal gardens as I was talking to Prince Morgan and little Purple Iris.

But as he got closer, another someone—someone to whom I most definitely did *not* want to speak ever again—stepped in the way.

"Olivia?" It was Lady Luisa Ferrari.

Of course she looked fabulous, as always, dressed in one of her Claudio gowns, this one in mint green.

Only this time there was something a little off about her. Her eyes were red-rimmed like she'd been

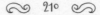

crying, and her grandmother, Baroness Bianca Ferrari, was at her side, her lips pressed very tightly together.

"Well," the baroness said, nudging Luisa in the side. "Say it."

Luisa shoved some of her perfectly straight hair from her shoulders and lifted her chin. "I'm sorry for what I did the last time I was here at the palace," she said. "And for the things I said to you. It was very wrong of me, and I hope you'll forgive me."

Just like that—Lady Luisa Ferrari had apologized!

I couldn't believe it. Luisa had never apologized for anything before in her life (at least to me)!

But she actually sounded like she meant it. She didn't *look* contrite (except for the red-rimmed eyes).

But she *sounded* sorry. Sorry she'd been caught, anyway.

"It's okay, Luisa," I said, mostly because I wanted to get to the person who was standing behind her, his hands in the pockets of his tuxedo trousers. Otherwise I would have stuck around to enjoy her apology more. "I forgive you."

Then Luisa did something that *really* astonished me. She stuck out her right hand.

"No," she said, in a more convincingly apologetic tone. "I really am sorry, Olivia. I said I was sorry to your sister, too. I never should have done what I did. I don't know why I act the way I do sometimes. Can we be friends again?"

I had never considered myself friends with Lady Luisa Ferrari in the first place.

But suddenly that didn't sound like such a terrible thing to be. We all grow and mature at our own rate. Maybe Luisa was finally catching up to me.

"Sure," I said, and shook hands with her . . . even though of course a part of me was totally suspicious of what she wanted. Continued unrestricted access to the palace of Genovia, so maybe next time she could steal the palace jewels?

It was possible.

But it was also possible that she was genuinely sorry, and really did want to be friends at last.

A true royal would give her the benefit of the doubt, so that's exactly what I did.

"Thanks," Luisa said, looking relieved as she pumped my hand up and down.

"You're welcome." Then I lowered my voice so that the baroness wouldn't overhear. "Hey, Luisa. Do you have a tampon I could borrow?"

She stopped pumping my hand, looking confused. "Wh-what?"

I started laughing. "Ha. Never mind." I raised my voice so that the baroness could hear me. "It was so lovely of you both to attend today's ceremony. Won't you step inside the dining room? I believe tea sandwiches and champagne are being served."

"Now, that," I heard the baroness say as they walked away, "is how a true princess behaves. You could learn a lot from that young lady, Luisa."

Luisa only grumbled something I couldn't hear, then whacked at a rosebush with her Claudio handbag.

That's when the best thing ever happened:

Prince Khalil stepped out from the shade of the palm tree under which he'd been standing and smiled at me.

"So are you and your cousin Luisa friends again?" he asked.

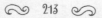

I shrugged, even though Grandmère says it is rude for princesses to shrug, especially when they're wearing off-the-shoulder gowns, which I happened to be wearing at that moment.

"She apologized," I said.

He raised those dark, thick eyebrows I have to admit I love so much. "And you forgave her?"

"It's the responsibility of a princess to be just and fair." Then I grinned. "Actually, I just wanted to get rid of her so I could talk to you. I saw you standing over there."

He grinned back. "That sounds just and fair to me. Anyway, here."

I looked down to see that he'd pressed a small, brightly colored cardboard box into my hand.

"What's this?" I asked, surprised.

"It's your gift," he said, seeming surprised that I was surprised. "The one I brought you from Paris. Open it."

"Oh." I'd sort of allowed myself to become convinced by Nishi that my gift was a kiss after all.

But of course it wasn't! How could I have been so

silly? It was something in a brightly colored little cardboard box that rattled a bit when I shook it.

"Don't shake it," Prince Khalil said. "You'll break it."

"Oops," I said. "Sorry. But Khalil, I didn't get you anything except that snake book because we promised we were only ever going to give each other books. And then I thought all those horrible things about you just because Luisa—"

"I know, I know," he said. "Let's never talk about that again. And I know about the books. But I went to Paris and saw this one thing and thought of you, and knew you had to have it. So open it."

Still feeling guilty, I opened the box's elaborate lid. I did not deserve a gift, especially from someone as sweet as Prince Khalil . . .

"You shouldn't have done this," I said as I worked the tabs to the box's lid. They were somewhat complicated, almost origami-like. "You know that—"

Then I saw what was inside the box, and almost burst out laughing.

"See?" Prince Khalil was grinning ear-to-ear as he saw my stunned—but pleased—reaction. "I knew you'd like it. But that's why I had to give it to you sooner than later. Any more time, and they'd all be stale."

Inside the box were six perfectly stacked macarons, each a different color of the rainbow.

"I know how much you love them," he went on excitedly. "And these are from a special shop in Paris. The pastry chef is supposed to be the best macaron baker in the world. And he makes them in really crazy flavors I just knew you'd want to try. I got you coffee, and tea, and bacon—can you imagine, a bacon macaron?—and bittersweet chocolate, and hazelnut, and—"

Before he could say another word, and before I lost my nerve—or the impulse—I reached up, wrapped an arm around his neck, and kissed him on the lips.

"Hey," he said softly, but not in a displeased way, when I pulled my face from his. He looked down at me with a confused expression on his face. "What was that for?"

"To say thank you," I said. "For giving me the best gift ever."

He looked even more confused. "Macarons?"

"Yes," I said. "Macarons."

But I didn't mean the macarons, of course. I meant his friendship . . . and his heart, which I could feel thumping against me.

And just like Mia vowed in the throne room, I mean to do everything I can from now on to protect it.

So I kissed him again, for good measure . . .

And he kissed me back!